D0969176

WITHDRAWN

SPECIAL MESSAGE TO READERS

This book is published under the auspices of

THE ULVERSCROFT FOUNDATION

(registered charity No. 264873 UK)

Established in 1972 to provide funds for research, diagnosis and treatment of eye diseases. Examples of contributions made are: —

A Children's Assessment Unit at Moorfield's Hospital, London.

•

Twin operating theatres at the Western Ophthalmic Hospital, London.

•

A Chair of Ophthalmology at the Royal Australian College of Ophthalmologists.

•

The Ulverscroft Children's Eye Unit at the Great Ormond Street Hospital For Sick Children, London.

You can help further the work of the Foundation by making a donation or leaving a legacy. Every contribution, no matter how small, is received with gratitude. Please write for details to:

THE ULVERSCROFT FOUNDATION,
The Green, Bradgate Road, Anstey,
Leicester LE7 7FU, England.
Telephone: (0116) 236 4325

In Australia write to:

THE ULVERSCROFT FOUNDATION,
c/o The Royal Australian and New Zealand
College of Ophthalmologists,
94-98 Chalmers Street, Surry Hills,
N.S.W. 2010, Australia

RETURN TO HEATHERCOTE MILL

Annis had vowed never to set foot in Heathercote Mill again. It held too many memories of her ex-fiancé, Andrew Freeman, who had died so tragically. But now her friend Sally was in trouble, and desperate for Annis' help with her wedding business. Reluctantly, Annis returned to Heathercote Mill and discovered many changes had occurred during her absence. She found herself confronted with an entirely new set of problems — not the least of them being Andrew's cousin, Ross Hadley . . .

Books by Jean M. Long
in the Linford Romance Library:

THE MAN WITH GRANITE EYES
CORNISH RHAPSODY
TO DREAM OF GOLD APPLES
ISLAND SERENADE
MUSIC OF THE HEART
BENEATH A LAKELAND MOON
JASMINE SUMMER
DESIGN FOR LOVING

JEAN M. LONG

RETURN TO HEATHERCOTE MILL

Complete and Unabridged

LINFORD
Leicester

First published in Great Britain in 2007

First Linford Edition
published 2008

British Library CIP Data

Long, Jean M.
Return to Heathercote Mill.—Large print ed.—
Linford romance library
1. Love stories
2. Large type books
I. Title
823.9′14 [F]

ISBN 978–1–84782–107–2

Published by
F. A. Thorpe (Publishing)
Anstey, Leicestershire

Set by Words & Graphics Ltd.
Anstey, Leicestershire
Printed and bound in Great Britain by
T. J. International Ltd., Padstow, Cornwall

This book is printed on acid-free paper

Annis Returns

Heathercote Mill was far more imposing than Annis remembered, and she stood for a moment, surveying the old building. The stone walls of the hotel were clad in Virginia creeper, which she knew would glow like rubies in the autumn.

Annis had spent many of her childhood holidays in the nearby village of Heronsbridge, staying at the home of her school friend, Sally Barnes. And later, after they'd both finished college, the two friends had worked together at Heathercote Mill, which at that time had been part-owned by Sally's uncle, Bryn Freeman.

A surge of emotions filled Annis as the memories flooded back.

A lot of those memories were happy ones, but some of them were tragic.

Suddenly the door swung open and

Sally Barnes was standing there, her pleasant face wreathed in smiles. The two friends hugged each other wordlessly.

'I saw you coming up the drive,' Sally said at last. 'Come on in!'

The hotel had certainly changed from when Annis had last been there and she couldn't help being impressed by the tastefully modernised reception area. She stood, looking around. Her feet sank into the deep pile of the mushroom-coloured carpet and the walls were a burnt orange, adorned by bright block prints and photographs of weddings that had taken place at the Mill in recent years.

Then Sally whisked her into an office gleaming with up-to-date equipment.

'You have no idea how relieved I am to see you,' Sally told her. 'It's been pandemonium here since Zoe left to have her baby. We had a temp, but she just wasn't suited to the job. Since then, I've been working all the hours that I can stay awake, trying to keep on top of things — and failing dismally.'

Annis laughed. 'You always were a dramatist, Sal. I don't believe a word of it, knowing how efficient you are. How are John and your Uncle Bryn?'

'John's away on a course — he had to be pushed into it by Ross. You know what my husband's like — totally unambitious. And Uncle Bryn's taken rather a back seat since the fire — he leaves most of it to Ross and Tristan these days.'

'Tristan?' Annis tried to put a face to the name.

'Tristan Marsden — Stella's brother. He came to work here soon after Uncle Arnold died and he's been here ever since.'

Sally looked uncomfortable, suspecting that her friend would react badly to this news. 'I suppose I should have mentioned it,' Sally said quietly.

Annis's expressive eyes widened. 'Yes, you should have. It could make things very awkward all round.'

Sally poured out coffee from the

bubbling percolator and passed the biscuit tin.

'I thought you wouldn't come if you knew,' she admitted.

'Well, I'm here now, so you'd better fill me in with what's been going on.' Annis nibbled on a chocolate digestive.

'Things aren't right, Annis. I can't quite put my finger on it, but . . . '

'You mean the business is going downhill?'

Sally shook her head, brown curls bouncing. 'No, quite the reverse. We're run off our feet. It's just that there have been a number of problems lately. Things happen that shouldn't, and every time, either Ross or Tristan seem to be around to sort things out.'

Annis frowned, unable to understand what her friend was getting at.

'But that's good, isn't it? Sally, you're not making sense.'

'That's because it's difficult to put into words.' Sally sighed. 'Annis, I'm positive that it's not my fault that all these mistakes are cropping up. And

Ross and Tristan seem to delight in scoring points off one another. One countermands what the other one says and it leads to confusion. On the surface, everything seems to run like clockwork, but it doesn't.'

Annis tried to get her head round all this. 'So, what does John think about it all?'

'Oh, you know John — laid back — never sees any wrong in anyone. There are times when I could shake him out of his complacency, but I love him to bits.'

'You're lucky to have such a lovely husband, Sally.'

'I know that, Annis, and I realise I ought to count my blessings when I think what happened to you . . . ' Sally felt a surge of sympathy for her friend.

At that moment the door opened and a man came into the room, tall and of medium build with thick, wavy, chestnut-brown hair and lean, good-looking features. Annis took one look at him and shot to her feet, her heart beating wildly.

'Andrew!'

But, of course, it wasn't Andrew. How could it be — Andrew was dead!

Annis gave a gasp and felt her legs crumple beneath her. She would have fallen to the floor but for a pair of strong arms that caught her and helped her back to her chair.

After a few moments she sat up shakily and smoothed back her hair. What a fool she'd made of herself. She took the glass of water that was held out to her.

'I'm so sorry — just for a moment, I thought . . . I thought . . . '

'I know what you thought,' said a harsh voice. 'Let me introduce myself. I'm Ross Hadley — Andrew's cousin. And I've no need to ask who you are. You're Annis Fuller, aren't you? What do you think you're doing here?'

'Wha — '

'I asked her to come,' Sally interjected. 'In case you hadn't noticed, I'm on my own in this office.'

Ross glared at Sally, dark eyes blazing. 'Then find another temp or get one of the other girls to cover — we employ enough of them. There must be someone to suit your requirements.' He turned back to Annis. 'I'm going to order some tea for you and then, when you're feeling better, I'd like you to leave.'

Annis gaped at him, shaken by his hostility towards her. 'But I've only just got here. Anyway, I'd like to see Bryn.'

There was a determined set to Ross's jaw.

'And that's precisely why I don't want you around. Mr Freeman isn't at all well these days. His shock at seeing you might be even greater than the one you've just received. You'll bring back too many memories for him. Sally, my office — now, please!'

From her perch on the rather hard chair, Annis could hear the drone of their two voices coming from the adjacent room, though she couldn't make out what they were saying. Her mind was in turmoil. Just for a fleeting moment, she'd thought that Ross Hadley was Andrew Freeman — her Andrew, who had been so cruelly killed in a fire at the Mill almost four years ago.

No, not *her* Andrew, she reminded herself. For, although Annis and Andrew were to have been married, only six weeks before the wedding he had called it off, saying that he had met someone else and had fallen in love with her.

The woman he had met was Stella Marsden — the granddaughter of Bryn Freeman's business partner, Arnold Marsden. Stella had, at that time, only recently returned to England from Canada and had been invited to come as a surprise guest to Arnold's seventy-fifth birthday party. Due to a bitter family dispute, Stella hadn't seen her grandfather for a number of years, but now the old gentleman was ill and he was desperate to make his peace before he died.

Within the space of three months,

Andrew and Stella were married, and then shortly after the wedding, Arnold Marsden had died.

* * *

Annis's thoughts were interrupted when, after a brief knock, a pretty, smiling girl in an overall came into the room carrying a covered tray. She set it out before Annis, gave her a shy smile and departed. Besides the tea, there was a tempting array of sandwiches, fruit and pastries, and in spite of herself Annis set to with an appetite, for she had missed lunch.

A few moments later, Sally returned. She gave Annis a big hug.

'Sorry about that, Annis. Are you feeling better now?'

Annis nodded. 'It was silly of me, but Ross looks so like Andrew at first glance.'

'I know, but he's not a bit like him, really. It's my fault that you got such a fright — I forgot you two hadn't met, even though you knew about each other from Andrew and myself. In fact, *everything's* all my fault. I can't seem to get anything right, lately.' Sally sighed. 'I've just been hauled over the coals for not consulting Ross before asking you to come down here. He says it's not viable for you to stay to help me out. I argued that we were a superb team before, and that although the Mill has expanded and we have more staff and equipment, the basic work is still very much the same.'

'But your argument fell on deaf ears?' Annis passed the cake, remembering Sally's sweet tooth.

Sally helped herself absently, and at Annis's invitation found a mug and poured some tea.

'Well, thanks for your support, Sally, but I'll not stay where I'm not wanted,' Annis said decisively. 'It was hard enough coming here in the first place.'

Sally had pleaded with Annis long and hard on the phone, persuading, cajoling, and finally convincing her that she would be welcomed at the Mill with open arms. Now, Sally opened her enormous hazel eyes wide in dismay.

'But you can't desert me now, Annis. I need your expertise.'

'But Ross doesn't. You heard what he said to you — you've obviously got a lot of staff here, any one of whom could help you, so why choose me?'

Sally ran a hand through her rather unruly mop of brown hair.

'You were always good at tackling problems, but it's not just that . . . ' She paused, looking almost frightened, Annis thought. 'Annis, listen — for ages now, I've suspected that there's been something going on behind my back, plans concerning the Mill that no-one's telling me about — probably because it's something I'd oppose . . . Look, Ross is going off-duty shortly until Monday, and in any case, you'll be staying with us at the cottage.'

'I *would* like the chance to see Bryn,' said Annis wistfully.

'OK, once Ross has gone, I'll go up

and see if Bryn feels he can see you. He's not been himself since the fire, you see. He feels guilty about it — as if he has no right to be here because Andrew died.'

'How can he blame himself?' Annis shook her head. 'It wasn't his fault, what happened. I heard that Andrew went back inside for Stella.'

'Yes — she'd managed to get out, but someone must have told him she was still inside . . . It was such a tragedy, such a waste.'

A kaleidoscope of memories flashed through Annis's mind — Andrew smiling up at her on a picnic by the river; the two of them walking hand in hand in a bluebell wood; dancing with him at numerous weddings held at the Mill . . . but destined never to dance with him at her own.

Sally looked at her friend with concern, aware of her suffering and not knowing how to help. She put a hand on Annis's arm.

'Look, why don't you go for a walk?'

she suggested. 'Just to get out of Ross's way. Leave your luggage here and come back in about an hour. He'll be gone by then, but just in case, I'll point out his car. It's a dark green Mercedes.'

Annis set off back down the drive in the direction of the village of Herons-bridge. It was difficult to believe that she hadn't been here for almost five years. In fact, it could have been just yesterday, especially when a young couple pushing a buggy stopped to talk to her.

'You're Annis Fuller, aren't you? How lovely to see you! You made our wedding day so very special. Everything was just perfect . . . This is our little girl.'

Annis bent to smile at the toddler and murmured something suitably approving, but she didn't really remember the couple. She had helped dozens of couples to have a perfect wedding — which was ironic when her own plans had gone so tragically wrong.

She walked along the High Street,

deep in thought.

Annis had worked at Heathercote Mill for several years and had been full of enthusiasm and ideas. Bryn Freeman and Arnold Marsden had been kind and considerate employers, and she had loved her job.

'Something Borrowed, Something Blue' had started off in a small way, but it had been Annis who had come up with the idea that, while the Mill was certainly a wonderful setting for weddings, they could offer so much more than just a venue. After all, there was enough to think about when you were getting married without having to cope with the hassle of getting it all to come together on the big day.

And so Annis had hit upon the idea of creating a complete package, arranging not just the reception but everything from the service onwards. They would hire out wedding outfits, liase with florists, bands, caterers — organize the whole day. But always allowing scope for people to make their own arrangements, and fitting in with them.

Word spread, and soon bookings were coming in fast and furious.

It was a tremendous success and then, just when things were at their peak, Arnold became ill and was forced to retire, although he continued to live at the Mill and to take an interest in the business.

Bryn was a widower with no children and so it was his great-nephew, Andrew Freeman, who came to help out, and Andrew with whom Annis fell so deeply in love. When they became engaged it had been the happiest day of her life and Bryn and Arnold had insisted that the wedding would be at Heathercote Mill — a complete package with no expense spared.

After Andrew broke off their engagement, Annis had left Heathercote Mill to stay with her parents in Dorset for a few months, before finding work in another hotel.

Andrew and Stella had married

almost immediately and, shortly afterwards, Arnold Marsden had died and Bryn Freeman had inherited the majority of his shares in the enterprise.

* * *

Annis glanced at her watch. It was still only half an hour since she'd left the Mill. She couldn't return just yet. She came upon a newly-opened antiques shop with a coffee bar and decided to while away the remainder of the time in there.

There were a couple of men talking animatedly in one corner and, after a quick glance at her, they lowered their voices. She took her time, looking at the items on display, which she thought were all rather pricey. Once or twice she glanced in the direction of the two men, wondering if they were dealers. The younger of the two was stocky but quite good-looking with thick sandy hair, whilst his companion was rather chubby and had a sly expression to his florid face.

After looking around the shop, she made her way to the coffee bar and ordered an over-priced cappuccino which she didn't really want.

She sat looking out into the attractive courtyard garden, wondering whatever had possessed her to return to Heronsbridge. She was already beginning to regret her decision, but at least she could stay long enough to reassure herself that Bryn was all right. She decided that she would stay with Sally for the weekend, and then return to London on Monday.

* * *

When she returned to Heathercote Mill, Annis was relieved to see that Ross Hadley's Mercedes was no longer in the carpark.

She went into the office just as Sally was putting down the phone, a frown creasing her normally good-natured features.

'We've a big wedding on tomorrow,'

she explained to Annis, 'and that was the bride's mother having a mega-panic. We can't afford for anything to go wrong, but I've got a nasty premonition that something will.'

'Why should it?' Annis was puzzled. Sally had always been so confident, but now she seemed very on edge.

'Because just lately *everything* always does go wrong, no matter how hard I check things out.'

'Then we'd better start to check and double check everything systematically now, before it's too late,' Annis said briskly. 'Let's look at your computer.'

Armed with phone numbers Annis set to work, saying that on this occasion she wasn't prepared to rely on e-mail or fax. She wanted to speak to people personally. Sally was extremely thorough and had already checked out a good deal of the items herself. The marquees were up, the caterers were ready for the following morning and so was the florist. It seemed as if there really couldn't be any last minute hitches . . . That was until they tried to contact the band and discovered that they had gone to Blackpool for the weekend!

'What did I tell you?' Sally wailed. 'This sort of thing happens all the time! I made the booking months ago! Now the agency says that it was cancelled a few weeks ago, but the girl can't remember who by. Annis, whatever are we going to do now? It's all down to me!'

'No, it's not because I'm here to help and we're going to sort this out.'

Annis thought hard. She began systematically phoning all the bands that the hotel regularly used, even though she was aware that unless one of them had a last- minute cancellation it would be impossible to find a substitute at this late stage.

After a fruitless half-hour, Annis turned to Sally.

'Look, I've got an idea. I can't promise anything, but would you be prepared to try someone completely new?'

Sally nodded. 'Beggars can't be choosers.'

Annis went ahead and contacted a friend of hers who had a young cousin desperate to get a break in the music world. Within the hour it was all set up.

Sally heaved a sigh of relief. 'There you are — I knew you'd sort things out. Mind you, we're not out of the woods yet. Ross will want to know why he wasn't consulted before we booked someone new.'

'Oh, he can go whistle,' Annis said rudely. 'Now, what's next?'

It seemed that everything else was in order, and as soon as they were sure of this, Sally went upstairs to her Uncle Bryn's flat, to return a few moments later with an invitation for Annis to join them.

* * *

Bryn Freeman had aged. The first thing Annis noted was his poor scarred hands, but his bright blue eyes lit up when he saw her and a smile crinkled his already lined face. She went across to the old gentleman and received a hug.

'Where have you been, lass? I've missed you so much,' he said.

Annis swallowed back the tears. 'I visited you in the nursing home after the — the fire,' she told him.

He sighed and took her hand. 'Yes, but that seems so long ago. You've lost weight, Annis. You're a mere shadow of yourself.'

She laughed. 'Go on with you, Bryn.'

'Well, it's wonderful to see you, lass. I keep thinking that if you and Andrew had stayed together none of this would have happened.'

'We can't turn back the clock,' she said gently, her heart aching. 'Sometimes people are just in the wrong place at the wrong time . . . '

He sighed again. 'I've never really cared for that Stella, but I do know that she loved my great-nephew. That's my one consolation . . . You didn't get to the funeral?'

'No — I didn't know about anything that had happened until after I returned from America.'

She had been in Virginia, visiting friends, and her family — in a bid to protect her, and knowing how much she needed the holiday — had thought it best to keep the news from her until her return. They had not realised how badly injured Andrew was, however, and he had died while Annis was away.

'I didn't get to the funeral either, because I was in hospital,' said Bryn quietly. 'He saved my life, you know.'

'I know,' Annis said gently, and bent to kiss the old man's cheek.

'Stella went away soon afterwards, to Canada to stay with her father — she couldn't face being here. But now she's back again.'

Sally had warned Annis that Stella had returned to Heronsbridge and this was something else that Annis was going to have to face up to.

'It's wonderful to see you, Annis. Stay as long as you like. I hope they've given you a nice room?' the old man asked.

'Oh, I'm staying with Sally and John for the time being. I wasn't sure if I'd be welcome.'

'Nonsense, girl. You'll always be welcome here. The place hasn't been the same without you, and Sally could do with a hand now that Zoe's left to have her baby.'

'But what about the other managers . . . Ross and Tristan?'

'Oh, they run the business, but I've got my finger on the pulse and I make sure I have the final say.' Bryn's blue eyes glinted. 'Ross protects me and Tristan tries to manipulate me, but at the end of the day, they know they have to respect my wishes because I control the finances and always have done. Now, don't you worry, you're to stay as long as you like. Move in here when you want to. Get Vicki on reception to organise it. Come and join me for dinner tonight — and Sally too; it'll save her cooking.'

They had a nostalgic evening, reminiscing about the Mill in the early days when it had first opened, and laughing over incidents from the past.

It was past ten o'clock when Sally and Annis left the Mill.

'I wish things could always be like that,' Sally remarked as they sat over a supper drink in her cottage. 'It was so relaxed. No pressure . . . Just like old times.'

Annis looked at her friend in surprise.

'That's not how I remember it — there was always pressure. It's that kind of job.'

'That's not what I mean, Annis. Oh, you'll find out soon enough what it's like if you stay around for any length of time. If it wasn't for Uncle Bryn, I'd have packed it all in long ago, but for his sake I feel I've got to make a go of it.'

'Come on, Sally, what is it?' Annis urged. 'Try to explain in words of one syllable what's bothering you?'

'That's just it — it's hard to put into words. After you left, Zoe came to work here and we got on fine. She'd never replace you, but she was a good substitute. Things went along on a fairly even keel for a while, and I suppose I was so immersed in my work and stunned by what had happened between you and Andrew that I kept myself to myself. Besides, Uncle Bryn was around to sort out any problems.'

Annis had pieced little bits together over the years from letters and e-mails and Sally had met up with her on the odd occasion in London and had a heart-to-heart. But then, after the fire, for a time they had ceased to communicate with one another, and this was apparently the point at which things had changed so radically.

'Go on,' Annis urged Sally.

'Stella used to swan about the place as if she owned it, but funnily enough — and I don't want to upset you by saying this — I don't dislike Stella. I think it genuinely was a chemistry thing between her and Andrew, and that — although I admit she appeared manipulative — it was just something that happened.'

Annis nodded. Hard as it was for her to accept what Sally said, she realised that it was the truth, and after all, now that Andrew had died, both she and Stella were in the same situation — except that Annis was the one that Andrew had rejected and Stella the one that he'd chosen to marry.

'Since the fire, nothing's been the same,' Sally explained to Annis. 'Ross turned up and was very supportive, and Tristan was here already, but suddenly they were both in control, and without realising it at the time I seem to have been . . . '

'Pushed out?' Annis suggested gently.

Her friend looked awkward. 'Yes, that's exactly how I feel — as if I'm here under sufferance. If anything goes wrong, it invariably seems to come back to me. Anyway, with you here to support me . . . '

Annis felt cornered. 'Sally, I can't promise anything. OK, I've taken a couple of weeks' holiday and the firm owes me so much leave I could probably stay on a bit longer, but I'd need to be very sure that I wanted to be here before I gave up my job.'

Sally nodded. 'I can understand that.' She sighed. 'I've tried to talk to John once or twice about how I feel about working here, but he seems to think I'm being paranoid. Of course, the easy thing to do would be to leave, but then I'd feel I was letting down Uncle Bryn and the rest of the team. If anyone can help me to sort out things here, it's you, Annis.'

* * *

Annis lay awake into the small hours, mulling over the events of the day in her mind. She was beginning to think she should have followed her instincts and stayed in London, but Sally had sounded so desperate on the phone and, somehow, Annis had felt a sudden urge to see Heathercote Mill again. However, now that she was here in Heronsbridge, she wasn't at all sure whether to stay or go.

They awoke to a glorious July day, just right for a wedding. The caterers and florists were hard at work from an early hour and so, unfortunately, was Mrs Lawrence, the bride's mother, who was determined to supervise the entire operation and get under everyone's feet.

Annis, as she tried to pour oil on troubled waters, wondered why Mrs Lawrence hadn't just organised it all herself in the first place.

A pretty, fluffy blonde, Mrs Lawrence was decidedly overwrought, and Annis acted quickly, shepherding her into the office and ordering coffee.

'Mrs Lawrence, everything is truly under control, so why not relax and leave it all to us?'

Mrs Lawrence sniffed into a lace-edged handkerchief. 'I was in hospital last year and my husband and daughter fixed this up so that I wouldn't have any worries, but now I feel superfluous. I wanted to be involved. She's my only daughter.'

'You know, we *are* a bit short-staffed,' said Sally, winking surreptitiously at Annis. 'I'm sure you could lend someone a hand, Mrs Lawrence. Perhaps you could check the seating plan and put out the place cards? They're so pretty, aren't they?'

It wasn't the first time they'd had to deal with an overwrought mother, and a pacified Mrs Lawrence went off in the direction of the marquee, much to the relief of Annis and Sally.

'We'll have to remember to send her packing around twelve o'clock or she'll never be ready for the ceremony,' Sally said.

It was around eleven o'clock when the office door was flung open and a stocky, sandy-haired young man entered. He pointedly ignored Annis and she suddenly remembered where she'd seen him before. It had been in the antiques shop the previous day; he'd ignored her then, too.

'There's a woman wandering around by the marquee,' he said to Sally.

'It's OK, it's the bride's mother. She's supposed to be there and she'll be going shortly. This is my good friend Annis Fuller by the way. She's helping me out for a week or two.'

As if noticing her for the first time, the young man turned to look at Annis and raised his eyebrows.

'I'm Tristan Marsden. I wasn't aware we'd taken on any new staff. Your name rings a bell.'

Annis met his hazel eyes levelly. 'I used to be engaged to Andrew.'

There was a silence for a moment or two as he digested this piece of information.

'But, of course — forgive me.' He stretched out a hand and she took it rather reluctantly.

'Annis and I go back a long way,' said Sally, getting to her feet. 'I'll leave you to get acquainted while I check on the caterers.'

To cover an awkward pause after Sally had gone, Annis said, 'It should be a good wedding. Everything's in hand and it's a glorious day.'

Tristan perched on the desk and flicked through the wedding folder.

'Mmn — has the cake arrived?'

'Yes, about an hour ago. Everything's going like clockwork.'

'You're nothing like I imagined,' he said suddenly.

Then he grinned, making her feel uncomfortable under his scrutiny.

'We all have preconceived ideas, don't we? Look, if you're going to be around here for a few days then perhaps we could have a meal together. After all, you might well have an axe to grind with my sister but that's no reason why we can't be friends.'

She caught her breath at his audacity, but then realised it would be a golden opportunity to find out more about what, if anything, was going wrong at

Heathercote Mill.

'OK, thanks, I'd like that — and, just for the record, I don't bear Stella any grudge. We both loved the same man — it was no-one's fault.'

She saw the undisguised look of surprise on Tristan's face and suspected that this was not what he had expected to hear from her.

He got to his feet. 'Yes, well, I must get on. I'm always a bit wary when things appear to be going too smoothly. Let's hope the bridegroom turns up, eh?'

Annis swallowed back a retort, hoping he wouldn't find out about the band, at least not until after they'd arrived and had a chance to perform.

* * *

Everything went like a dream. It was a church wedding and so there was a little more time to prepare than if the ceremony had taken place at the Mill. Once the reception was in full swing,

Sally breathed a sigh of relief and she and Annis ate a late lunch in the office.

'There used to be a time when I could leave someone else in charge for an hour or so and slip over to the staff restaurant, but I daren't do that these days, because you can bet that if I do, something will go wrong.'

'Not today, surely? It's all gone splendidly so far.'

Tristan came in at that point. 'Everyone seems fairly happy. Just one or two minor glitches.'

Sally visibly paled and Annis found it difficult to believe her ears.

'What glitches?' Sally asked.

'Well, it seems the buttonholes weren't quite right, and although the Lawrences aren't aware of it, they've been served a more expensive champagne, so — since it's our mistake — we'll have to pick up the tab.'

Sally looked stunned. She looked at the wedding folder and then turned to check the information on the computer screen. She frowned.

'There doesn't appear to be any discrepancy here. They both say the same and . . . '

Tristan interrupted her. 'They may well do, but it's the wrong champagne and it came from a box with the name Lawrence on it. You must surely have signed for it before it went into the cellars? Anyway, it's too late to do anything about it now. I'll see you later.'

As the door closed behind him, Sally pulled a face.

'However do you put up with him?' Annis asked.

'Oh, I'm used to him by now. Like I said, I only stay for Uncle Bryn's sake and because I can see something of John during the day,' Sally said, looking thoroughly miserable. 'All I've ever wanted was just to get on and do my job, but I don't seem to be able to do anything right as far as Tristan and Ross are concerned.'

A New Challenge

To everyone's relief, the rest of the day passed off without any further hitches. The band had proved a great success, and the wedding had been thoroughly enjoyed by all concerned. Annis and Sally returned to the cottage feeling tired but pleased with themselves.

Sally and John lived in a pretty cottage built of Kentish ragstone, with honeysuckle and roses climbing its walls.

'You know,' said Annis, curled up on the sofa in the comfortable sitting-room, enjoying a cup of coffee, 'there are still a few things I've never understood. At the time, because of what happened between myself and Andrew, I didn't want to know the answers, but now . . . '

Sally frowned. 'Annis, you're the one not making sense now. Tell me what you don't understand.'

'Well, how was it that Stella was invited to Uncle Arnie's party in the first place? I never knew how anyone managed to track her down.'

'It was Ross who invited her. They were childhood friends. The whole family had originally come from up north, remember?'

Annis nodded, listening intently to what her friend had to say.

'Uncle Arnie and Uncle Bryn didn't move to Heronsbridge until they both became widowers. They'd been involved in business ventures before, but nothing like the Mill.

'When Uncle Arnie's son, Kevin, and his wife split up, Stella and Tristan were still at school. It made sense for them to finish their schooling in England, but afterwards they chose to join their father in Canada. Who could blame them? It was a new and exciting life.'

'Go on,' Annis urged as Sally paused to sip her coffee.

'Ross always had a soft spot for Stella

and kept in touch. Uncle Arnie had fallen out with Kevin, as you know, but he longed for a reconciliation with his family before he died, and so when his seventy-fifth birthday party was being planned, Ross contacted Stella who was back in England by then. He told her how ill her grandfather was and so she came to see him.'

'So why didn't she come sooner?' Annis asked.

'I don't know, you'd have to ask her that. But remember, Annis, her father had prejudiced her against her grandfather.'

'So what about Tristan? Did he manage to see Arnold before he died?'

Sally shook her head. 'Sadly, no. He didn't put in an appearance until afterwards.'

Sally's ginger cat, George, jumped on to Annis's lap, purring loudly and she stroked him absently.

'So Tristan wasn't even at Stella and Andrew's wedding?'

'No, he was travelling around the

world at the time. And before you ask, no, Kevin wasn't there either. But Stella's mother, Audrey, was. She's a very nice lady.'

'I see.' Annis helped herself to a biscuit. There were suddenly so many unanswered questions, and so much to think about.

'And what about Kevin Marsden? I'm surprised he didn't come back here to claim his rightful inheritance after his father died.'

Sally leaned back in her chair, pleased that at last Annis was showing an interest in the situation at Heathercote Mill.

'Well, he'd just remarried — and his new wife was a wealthy widow by all accounts. Anyway, he was hardly cut off without a brass farthing. From what I can gather, although Kevin wasn't given a share of the Mill, Uncle Arnold left him some property in Yorkshire. Arnold also left a generous trust fund for Stella and Tristan. Like the rest of us, they've also got shares in the company, although, of course, Uncle Bryn inherited the lion's share.'

Annis mulled all this over.

Presently, she helped Sally prepare supper and, as they sat over a leisurely lasagne and salad, she wondered if Sally really knew all that had been going on over the past few years.

'There is something else I've been wondering about. What about Ross? In all the years I stayed in Heronsbridge, I didn't once see Ross. How come he suddenly appeared on the scene when he did? Why had he never been to visit Bryn before?'

'Annis, there's nothing shady about Ross,' said Sally. 'What you've got to realise is that both he and Stella are a few years older than us. They were both through school and university, and out into the big wide world, living overseas, when we stayed here. On the other hand, Andrew was living in London, so when Uncle Arnold became ill, he was the obvious choice to help Uncle Bryn run the company.'

Annis nodded. 'Yes, I realise all that. Andrew didn't mention the others much. He was a bit younger than them, wasn't he?'

'Three years younger than Ross, who's around thirty-five, and about eighteen months younger than Stella. That's why you saw Andrew at Heronsbridge when you stayed, of course, because his family lived abroad by then and he came here for his holidays, like you did. More lasagne?'

Annis passed her plate. Sally was a good cook and the meal was delicious.

There was a lot to think about and they fell silent for a time. Annis wondered if somewhere, in all this, there was a clue to all the problems that Sally had encountered recently.

Presently, Sally got to her feet and began to collect up the dishes.

'Well, I think I've told you most things now. Ready for dessert?'

The conversation turned to lighter topics and Sally visibly relaxed, but Annis was still worried about her. There were dark smudges under her eyes and she wasn't her usual cheerful self.

'You've no idea how much better I feel now that you're here, Annis,' Sally told her. 'If anyone can get to the bottom of what's going on around here, you can. I've missed you so much these past few years and it doesn't sound to me as if things are working out for you in London.'

Annis grimaced. 'I used to love my job, but a change of management has altered all that.' She caught Sally's sympathetic glance and suddenly burst out laughing. 'What a pair we are — both having problems with our jobs and letting it get to us. Well, it's high time we did something about it. Let's begin with yours. You know how I like a challenge and we've always worked well together in the past, so I'm sure if the two of us put our heads together we can sort out whatever's wrong here.'

Annis had decided that sorting out things at Heathercote Mill would certainly be a challenge, but not beyond her capabilities. Sally had every confidence in her ability to tackle the problem and Annis didn't want to let her friend down.

* * *

Sunday was a pleasant day. Sally and Annis went to visit Sally's parents who now lived in a small town about six miles away from Heronsbridge. After joining them for the morning service at the local church, Sally and Annis went back with them for lunch at their bungalow.

Sally's mother was Bryn's cousin, but was a great deal younger than him. A plump, round-faced little woman with grey hair and a ready smile, Mrs Morrison had been like a second mother to Annis during the time that her own parents had been abroad. They had a lot of catching up to do and they chatted away as they ate excellent roast lamb followed by apple pie.

It was late afternoon before Sally and

Annis returned to Heronsbridge and they sat out in the colourful little cottage garden, enjoying the sunshine. Annis had dreaded coming back, but realised that after the smoke of the city, it was good to be in the Kentish countryside again. She inhaled the perfume from a multitude of blooms and sighed contentedly. John was a talented gardener and was in charge of the grounds at Heathercote Mill.

'OK, so fill me in,' she said presently, as they drank yet more cups of tea. 'If I'm going to work with you, I'll need to know every last detail about the day-to-day running of the Mill. Update me. I need to get my head round things and quickly, if I'm to be of any use to you at all tomorrow.'

Sally stretched out on the sun lounger and thought about this.

'Well, I suppose it isn't that much different since you were here last, but there have been some changes, as you would expect. I'll run through the main things when we're in the office.'

'And you'd better explain the roles Tristan and Ross play.'

'Oh, that's pretty straightforward. They handle the finances and marketing and generally keep their fingers on the pulse. Although, in the main, they're based in the conference centre, they oversee the day-to-day running of the entire enterprise. Everything has to be approved by one or the other, but Uncle Bryn is still at the helm. Anything major still has to be authorised by him, and he can and does veto things if necessary.'

Annis was a little surprised that Sally was taking such a back seat.

'Sounds as if you have a lot less responsibility than before,' she commented now, watching for Sally's reaction, but Sally's expression gave nothing away.

'Well, yes, but sometimes that's a good thing,' she said.

Annis bent down to stroke George, who was lying beside her on the grass. She chose her words carefully.

‘Has it ever occurred to you that someone might be deliberately setting out to make life difficult for you?’ she asked.

Sally’s eyes widened. ‘What possible motive could they have? No, I’m sure you’re wrong there,’ she said, reaching for her cardigan. ‘Now, I think we ought to arrive at work early tomorrow and make sure we’ve got Uncle Bryn’s blessing for you to begin work before the others get wind of what’s happening. Actually, come to think of it, it’ll only be Ross on duty because Tristan’s got the day off.’

‘OK, we’ll see how it goes, shall we?’ said Annis, nodding and making a rapid decision. ‘And I’ll see if I can figure out what — if anything — is going on. But I’m only prepared to give it ten days’ trial, Sally. If I don’t feel any more welcome by the end of that time, then I’ll have no alternative but to return to London. Remember, officially I’m only on leave!’

Sally nodded, aware that her friend

would do her best to help her.

'That's fair enough.' She scrambled to her feet. 'It's getting chilly. Shall we go inside? There's a DVD I thought you might like to watch after supper.'

* * *

Monday dawned bright and clear, and Annis got up deciding to enjoy herself, regardless of what might happen. Determined to make a good impression, she dressed in a neat black suit and a crisp white blouse, securing her hair with a slide.

'This morning should be quite straightforward,' Sally told her over breakfast. 'Two lots of parents to be interviewed with their daughters. In other words, the hard sell. The first meeting isn't until ten though, so there will be plenty of time for you to see Uncle Bryn before then, while I catch up on some paperwork.'

'And what services do you offer nowadays?' Annis helped herself to toast and marmalade.

'There are around ten different packages available, with various permutations. And for any cancellations, there's a returnable amount on a sliding scale for up to a month before the wedding.'

'And what if it's a very late cancellation?'

Sally shrugged. 'Zilch, I'm afraid, unless there are extenuating circumstances. We've got to think about overheads. It's a hard-line tactic, I know, but after all, we are a business and . . . '

'There's no sentiment in business. What a pity! It's not how it used to be in the old days.'

Annis was disappointed that 'Something Borrowed, Something Blue' had apparently turned into such an impersonal and mercenary enterprise during her absence.

'OK,' she said. 'So how about if I sit in on the interviews, take a few notes and generally try to get the feel of things — how would that be?'

'Sounds good to me. I'll just feed George, and then, when you're ready, we'll be off.'

When Annis went to see Bryn Freeman there was a young girl sitting on a footstool, chatting to him while he drank his coffee. It was the same girl who had brought Annis her tea on Friday. She got to her feet as Annis entered the room. She was petite and extremely pretty with dark hair and expressive brown eyes.

'Hello, Annis — this is Camille, Madame Cecile's daughter. She's helping in the kitchen during the holidays and has brought me my coffee. Millie, this is Annis Fuller — a friend of Sally Barnes.'

They exchanged greetings and then Millie said, 'I'm supposed to find out what you want for your lunch, Mr Freeman, before I go back to the kitchen.'

'Well, I'd better tell you then, else Chef will not be pleased!'

Millie smiled as he ticked the menu card and handed it back to her, then she said a polite goodbye to Annis and left the room.

'Charming girl,' Bryn said. 'She's like a breath of fresh air.'

'You said she's Madame Cecile's daughter — who's Madame Cecile?' Annis asked.

'Oh, haven't you met her yet? She runs the boutique in the new complex. She makes the most exquisite wedding gowns. Actually, she's a sort of cousin of mine — at least, her late husband's father was my wife's cousin. Work that one out!'

'I'll do my best,' Annis promised him, aware of how much store he set by his family, however distant the relationship.

'Now, what did you want to see me about, Annis?' Bryn's blue eyes studied her keenly.

She came straight to the point. 'I wondered how you'd feel about my staying on to help Sally for a week or two — on a voluntary basis, of course.

I've got some leave to use up and . . . '

Bryn reached out and took her hands between his.

'Annis, you're welcome to stay for as long as you want. You're like a member of my family too, and I'm delighted you've come to visit. I know things have changed since you were last here — not all of them for the better — but I haven't. Just you remember that, my dear. You must stay for as long as you wish, with my blessing! And if you want to move into the staff wing, then I'll arrange for a room to be made available whenever you say the word.'

She thanked him and refused his offer of coffee, but stayed talking to him for a few more minutes. Before leaving, she reached across and added a few pieces to the large jigsaw puzzle on the table.

Bryn chuckled. 'Come and see me again, lass, and don't work too hard. I know you of old, remember!'

* * *

Sally was busy at the computer when Annis went into the office.

'I've just met Madame Cecile's daughter. What a pretty girl.'

'She is, isn't she?' Sally smiled. 'She took Uncle Bryn's coffee up one day and chatted for a few minutes and now she's got into the habit of visiting. He's taken quite a shine to her. He looks upon her as the granddaughter he never had. Sometimes she takes a group of her young friends up to see him.' Sally leaned back in her chair.

'Actually, there's quite a story attached to young Millie. She's still at school studying for her 'A' levels but she works here during the holidays and helps her mother in the boutique on her afternoon off. You haven't seen the boutique yet, have you? We'll take a look this afternoon. Madame Cecile makes the most gorgeous wedding gowns. They're absolutely out of this world. The thing is, Millie's a very talented dancer and really wants to work in the theatre, but her mother won't hear of it. She wants Millie to do an Art and Design course so that she can help her in the boutique when she qualifies.'

Annis's eyes widened. 'But surely, in this day and age . . . '

'Exactly — and there's more. Millie is going out with one of the waiters. He's at university and works here in the holidays. He's doing a performing arts course and . . . '

'And I suppose Madame Cecile opposes the relationship?'

Sally nodded. 'She certainly does, because it doesn't fit in with her ambitious plans for her daughter! The staff are very much on the side of the young couple. Dean's a nice lad and Millie works her socks off in the kitchen, getting the money together to take her to university.'

Annis helped herself to some coffee and perched on Sally's desk.

'How old is she? She must be around seventeen? She's able to make her own decisions, so why doesn't she stand up for herself?'

'Oh, she's very loyal to her mother. Madame Cecile's a widow and she's had quite a struggle to bring up Millie by herself. Millie obviously doesn't want to upset her. Anyway, she's got Uncle Bryn firmly on her side too, so we'll see. They're sort of related and you know how he feels about family.'

* * *

The first part of the morning was very pleasant. The two brides-to-be and their parents, although both delightful, were very different.

Money seemed to be no object for the family of the first young lady, but the second family were obviously on an extremely tight budget.

After both families had gone, Annis and Sally sat discussing them.

'So, what are your first impressions, Annis?'

'Well, they're both going to be challenging in their own way, aren't they? The first one because it has to be original and the second one because it's being done on a shoestring.'

'And I bet I know which one you'd prefer . . . ' Sally trailed off, looking awkward, and Annis, who could read her friend like a book, said, 'It's OK, Sal, I've put the past behind me. There's no need to tread softly. I'll always miss Andrew and it'll be a long time before I get romantically involved with anyone else, but that doesn't mean I can't take an interest in other people's wedding arrangements.'

The door was suddenly and unceremoniously flung open and Ross Hadley stood there, a frown furrowing his handsome brow.

'Here you are, Sally. Have you forgotten our meeting?'

Sally jumped to her feet, looking flustered.

'Is it that time already? Of course I haven't forgotten, Ross, but our clients have only just gone. Both families made firm bookings, by the way.'

'Good! That's how it should be.'

Then he noticed Annis.

'What are you still doing here, Miss Fuller? I thought you'd gone back to London?'

Annis fixed him with an innocent stare from her long-lashed eyes.

'Mr Freeman has invited me to stay for as long as I choose. If you have any objection to that, Mr Hadley, then I suggest you raise the issue with him.'

Ross's face darkened. 'Well, we'll see about that,' he said icily. 'I'm just about to speak with Mr Freeman. Now, Sally — five minutes — no longer, please!'

'Well, he's all sweetness and light this morning, isn't he?' Annis commented, as the door closed behind him.

'I'm so sorry, Annis.' Sally looked miserable. 'It can't be very pleasant for you, all this bad feeling.'

'It's not your problem, Sal. Anyway, while you're away, how about I go through all the information you've put on the computer this morning and check it against what you've written in the book. I think it would be a good idea if I start double-checking everything over the course of the next couple of weeks or so?'

'Would you, Annis?' Sally looked relieved. 'It would take a great weight off my mind. Hopefully you can pick up on any errors before it's too late. Anyway, I'd better fly, before I get into trouble again!'

Seeing Around The Mill

For the next forty-five minutes, Annis systematically checked the files against the computer. Bryn had always insisted that the information should be in two places as he had never trusted computers, and Annis was glad to see that this practice was still being maintained.

After going through all the entries for that day's clients, and not coming across a single mistake, she leafed through the entry book again.

A big conference was being held during the week and so only one wedding was listed for that Saturday, and Sally had told Annis that while Ross and Tristan usually dealt with the conferences themselves, she would sometimes help them out if she were free.

Suddenly the office door crashed open and Ross Hadley came storming in to stand towering over Annis with a face like thunder.

'What on earth's going on here? Why are you sitting at Sally's desk, using her computer?'

'Sally has far too much work and I'm giving her a hand. She's my friend and I care about her, even if you don't,' she replied coldly.

His brown eyes swept over her.

'Tell me, Miss Fuller — exactly why did you come back here?'

'I came to see Sally, John and Bryn,' she replied reasonably, resolving to remain outwardly calm, even though she didn't feel it.

'But why now? After all this time?' he persisted.

'I have rather a lot of leave to use up and thought it was high time I paid my friends a visit. Actually, I've had a bit of a problem plucking up the courage to return before now.'

A flash of sympathy passed across his face.

'Yes, I can appreciate that. It must

have been a difficult time for you — as indeed it was for all of us. We were all affected, but we've had to move on.'

She nodded. 'Yes, and I think I've done just that.'

He pulled up a chair. 'Mr Freeman tells me you've offered to act as some kind of assistant to Sally in a voluntary capacity . . . Why would you want to do that?'

'I would have thought that was obvious.' She glared at him. 'Sally is overworked and so I'm lending a hand until she's caught up with the backlog — it's as simple as that.' She watched his face as she added. 'Also, she seems to have been having a lot of problems lately, and I thought I might just be able to help sort out any glitches before they manifested themselves.'

'Act as a troubleshooter, you mean?' His eyes narrowed. 'So you're prepared to accept that your friend has been making a lot of mistakes lately?'

'Is anyone infallible, Mr Hadley? Sally and I go back a long way. It's obvious she's been under a lot of pressure lately and so, if I can help her to get back on her feet, then I will.'

'Very commendable!' He glanced at the computer screen. 'And have you discovered any mistakes?'

Annis was aware that he was trying to catch her off guard and said coolly, 'It would be disloyal to discuss that with anyone apart from Sally, don't you think?'

He gave a little laugh. 'What I think is that you're an interfering female with time on her hands. Don't you have a life of your own?'

He saw her pained expression and realised that he had touched a raw nerve.

'I'm sorry, that was unforgivable. Look, if you're going to stay around for a bit, then I suppose we should make an effort to get on with one another.'

He held out his hand and she took it reluctantly. She was totally unprepared for the frisson that shot down her spine at the contact and let go as if she'd been stung.

He shot her a look of irritation.

'OK, there's no need to make it so clear that you dislike me. Perhaps the feeling's mutual, but we'll just have to make the best of it, won't we?'

Annoyed with herself for reacting in the way she had, Annis turned her attention back to the computer.

In order to discover if there were any future plans for the Mill that didn't include Sally, she realised that she would need to befriend both Ross and Tristan. She decided that she would have to let them think she believed that Sally was capable of making the mistakes. Perhaps then they would admit that they were trying to get rid of Sally.

Glancing up, she found Ross looking at her intently, head on one side, as if he couldn't quite sum her up. She made a supreme effort.

'I'm sorry, Mr Hadley. I think we've got off on the wrong footing. I'm rather hungry and that always makes me irritable — any chance I could get some lunch?'

Ross immediately looked contrite. 'Actually I haven't eaten either. I'll ring the kitchen.' He picked up the phone.

'So, where's Sally?' Annis asked, when he'd finished the call.

'Oh, didn't I say? She's had to relieve one of the staff on reception — emergency dental appointment. These things happen from time to time, and Sally steps in. Actually I came to collect some invoices. They're on her desk, she said.'

He leaned across and rummaged in the tray, and she was again aware of his closeness.

'Ah, here they are!' He straightened up. 'So what's on the agenda for this afternoon? Has Sally put you in the picture?'

'It's all in here.' Annis indicated the diary. 'We were planning to start setting up the two weddings that were booked this morning. And Sally wants to take me to the shopping complex to show me around the dressmaker's. We're going to book fittings appointments for one of our brides while we're there.'

Ross glanced at the diary. 'So what's wrong with e-mail and the phone?'

'Nothing. Sally just thought I'd like to see the boutique for myself and to be introduced to Madame Cecile.'

'Yes, I see. OK, you can go ahead and do that, then. How far have you got with the details of the new bookings?'

She showed him the list and he ran his eye over it.

'Yes, that seems in order. So far so good. There is just one thing, Miss Fuller — I was checking through some invoices with Mr Freeman this morning and came across one from the band that was used for Saturday's wedding. I don't recognise the name. You wouldn't know what happened to the original group that were booked, by any chance?'

She had been waiting for this and was prepared.

'They let us down at the eleventh

hour,' she replied, not meeting his gaze. 'We had difficulty finding a replacement, but this group was very good and there were plenty of compliments.'

'I see, and apparently they were cheaper. Were you instrumental in arranging them?'

She couldn't help laughing at the unintentional pun and he joined in.

'Yes, as a matter of fact, I did recommend them.'

'Right, so you bailed Sally out. I hope she was grateful.'

Annis felt the anger rising in her. 'Why should Sally need to be grateful? How could it be her fault if the original band let her down?'

'She's in charge of this department, so if anything goes wrong she has to take responsibility. However, thanks to you, it seems we managed to avoid yet another crisis.'

This man was unbelievable! No wonder Sally was having such a hard time of it, if this was what she had to contend with.

Annis bit back a sharp retort and turned her attention back to the computer. Fortunately, there was a knock on the door at that point and Millie appeared with a covered tray.

'Thanks, Millie, you're a star!' Ross cleared a space on the desk and took it from her with a smile. 'Tuck in, Miss Fuller, there's quite a good selection — probably leftovers from Saturday's wedding. What do you take in your tea?'

'Just milk, please.'

She studied him as he poured the tea and wondered how she could ever have thought he was like Andrew. Yes, there was a striking similarity in looks, but there the resemblance ended. His manner and nature were totally different. Andrew had been charming with a wonderful sense of humour, whereas Ross Hadley was arrogant, impersonal, and coolly polite.

He passed her tea and gave her a sharp look, as if she had spoken her thoughts aloud.

'There have been a number of

necessary changes since you last worked here, Miss Fuller. I think you'll find we're more upmarket nowadays. We run a much tighter ship and we don't have room for negligent personnel. We have a reputation to uphold. Now, help yourself to the food and tell me a bit about yourself.'

Annis bit into a chicken sandwich hungrily.

'I would have thought you'd have found out all you need to know already. There's really very little to tell,' she said coolly.

'Maybe you could fill in some gaps for me then. You're very good friends with Sally. How did that come about? Did you live in Heronsbridge at one time?'

'No, Sally and I met at boarding school. My parents worked abroad a lot of the time and during the holidays I would either come here to stay with Sally and her parents, or else Sally would come out to Africa with me to visit my family. We've been friends ever since. We went to different colleges and met up from time to time, and then Sally came here to work for her Uncle Bryn after she qualified. I joined her shortly afterwards.'

Ross finished his sandwiches and reached for an apple.

'And whose idea was it to hold weddings here?' he asked.

'Bryn's initially, but it was me who came up with the idea of having a complete package, and then Sally and I worked out a plan which both Bryn and Arnold approved. Why?'

He shrugged. 'No particular reason — I'm just curious to know how it came about.'

In a lightning flash, Annis suddenly realised why Tristan and Ross might not be so keen for the wedding business to prosper. If 'Something Borrowed, Something Blue' was bringing in more money than the conference centre, then the two ambitious young men might not be happy for Sally to steal their thunder.

'So, are you planning to change things?' Annis asked.

'Why on earth would I want to do that — even if it were in my power to do so?' He gave her a keen look.

She shrugged, realising that she would have to tread carefully. 'I have the feeling that even though they bring in a lot of revenue for the hotel, organizing weddings is not your cup of tea.'

He smiled. 'I'll admit it's hardly my forte and it's certainly not Tristan's, but we're quite happy to run the conference centre — which is also fairly lucrative — and leave the weddings for Sally to sort out.'

Annis wasn't convinced, but was determined not to let him see this.

'That's OK then. I suppose weddings are more a woman's thing — at least, as far as the organization of them is concerned.'

Ross got to his feet and scooped up the invoices.

'You could be right. Well, if you're

ready, shall we go and take a look at the new complex? It looks as if Sally's going to be detained for a bit longer and I've got a spot of free time just now.'

He opened the door for her and, as she swept past, she caught the scent of his cologne — fresh and woody.

* * *

The new complex, situated at the rear of the Mill, was comprised of a series of separate units. Madame Cecile's boutique was one of these units and was light and spacious with deep-pink carpets and pearly-grey walls.

'Good afternoon, Madame, I've brought Miss Annis Fuller to see you. She's a friend of Sally Barnes and is helping her out for a week or two.'

Madame Cecile was a small, birdlike woman of indeterminate age, dressed in black with her dark hair scraped back in a chignon. She greeted Annis politely and showed her proudly around the shop, introducing her to her assistant,

Lara Henderson.

Madame Cecile gave Lara the new appointments to write into the diary while Annis admired a beautiful, ivory satin gown with a scattering of rosebuds and tiny teardrop pearls.

Then Annis followed Madame Cecile into an adjoining room where there were a variety of bridal gowns and bridesmaids' dresses, both for hire and for sale.

In a smaller room there were rows of gentlemen's suits, waistcoats, cravats and top hats, also for sale or for hire.

The quality of workmanship was exceptional, and Annis was very impressed.

After leaving the boutique, Ross took Annis to see a little shop which was opened during conferences only. He produced the key and they went inside.

'Just the usual stationery supplies, biscuits, sweets, canned drinks and a few things the delegates might forget. There's a printers' shop just along there, but it's closed at the moment so let's go back to the Mill and take a look at the new kitchen.'

Annis found the tour interesting, but was frankly amazed at the way the business had escalated since she had worked there last. It was now on such a large scale that it seemed to be in danger of losing its personal touch.

The old kitchen had been seriously damaged in the fire and the new one was state of the art and — in keeping with health rules and regulations — a gleaming sea of stainless steel.

She was pleased to see more than one familiar face in the kitchen, including Millie's, and she stopped to exchange a few words with Luis — who Annis knew from working here before, and who was now head chef. Preparations were underway for dinner that evening, and so Annis and Ross didn't stay too long.

Shortly afterwards, Ross was called away and so Annis made her way back to the office alone to discover Sally beavering away at the computer.

'So there you are, Annis. I was starting to worry about where you'd got to! I was beginning to think you'd taken a train back to London!'

'Ross was showing me around the new complex. You look shattered, Sally. I bet you haven't had any lunch.'

'Well, I did manage to grab a sandwich and half a cup of cold coffee. But I'm disappointed to hear you've had a tour of the complex already. I wanted to show you round myself and see your reaction.'

'Oh, sorry.' Annis cleared a pile of files from a chair and sat down. 'It's certainly impressive, I'll grant you. I've still to see the printers' shop though, because it was closed.'

'Oh, yes, it would have been. Jeff's been in the conference centre sorting out some graphics, but he's back now — I've just rung him,' Sally told Annis. 'I tell you what, let's go over there right now. You can have a look around the shop and then we can cadge some coffee off Jeff. Chef's given me some lovely cakes. We'll have them down by the lake. I reckon we've earned a bit of free time.'

* * *

Annis found the printers' shop fascinating. She double-checked some orders that Sally had placed for a variety of different types of wedding stationery, and was amazed at the choice available for invitation and place cards, napkins, orders of service, etc.

Jeff Hughes ran the enterprise along with his brother, Alan, and they were also on hand during conferences to give on-the-spot help and advice with the conference centre's computers.

As Sally and Annis left the shop carrying their paper cups of coffee, Sally remarked, 'Jeff used to work for a firm which required him to travel abroad a lot, but he was taken quite seriously ill and needed a quieter lifestyle. This suits him admirably.'

'Yes, he seems a nice guy. He's

certainly got a wide range of products there!'

⋆ ⋆ ⋆

They had reached the mill pond which nowadays was more like a small lake fed by a stream. It was a pretty area, recently landscaped and surrounded by trees. Sadly, there was nothing remaining of the original mill after which the present house had been named, although there was a rather nice engraving of it hanging in the hotel reception area.

The mill pond was a sheltered spot with several attractive wrought iron benches. Sally and Annis sat down to watch the ducks and other water fowl while they enjoyed their coffee and cakes.

'I've got something to tell you, Sally,' Annis said presently.

'So, come on, Sherlock, what have you come up with?'

'Oh, not a lot. I can't throw any light

on the problems you've been encountering. But something that Ross said got me thinking. It's not much to go on, I'll admit, but I just wondered . . . '

'What?' Sally reached for an éclair.

'Ross was asking whose idea it had been to go into the wedding business and I suddenly realised that perhaps this was at the root of things. It made me wonder whether 'Something Borrowed, Something Blue' maybe isn't popular with everyone at Heathercote Mill. It is rather a female-orientated business, after all.'

Sally frowned as she finished off the éclair and selected a rum truffle.

'I'm not sure what you're driving at, Annis. 'Something Borrowed, Something Blue' might not have been Ross and Tristan's choice, but they weren't around when it started up, were they? And it was Uncle Bryn's idea initially, if you remember. Anyway, Andrew was certainly keen on it, as you know. No, I'm afraid I don't go along with that.'

'Well, it's just a theory.' Annis stared

unseeingly at the lake. 'But I got to thinking that perhaps there might be other plans for the mill that don't include the wedding business and that's why you've been getting pushed out. I mean, all this expansion — exactly who was involved in that?'

'Well, all of us, I suppose. You would have been informed yourself as a shareholder. Andrew and Stella certainly both thought it was an excellent idea. I still can't see where you're coming from.'

'Probably because you're too close to things. Has it occurred to you that there could be other — potentially more profitable — business schemes than the wedding business?' Annis swept her arms about her. 'There's a lot of ground here and I'm wondering if someone might have earmarked all this for something else.'

Sally stared at her in amazement. 'Such as?' she queried.

Annis shook her head. 'Oh, I don't know. But if Bryn were persuaded to sell up or diversify — use the land for houses, perhaps, or a superstore . . . Look, I've probably got it all wrong . . . '

Sally shook the crumbs from her lap. 'Let's hope so. I'm beginning to think I shouldn't have involved you. After all, you haven't shown much interest in the place in recent years, have you?'

Annis was taken aback by her friend's reproachful tone. 'Come on! You know the reason for that!'

But then she thought about what Sally had said.

'OK, I suppose I deserved that. But tell me, Sal, who else apart from you and Bryn knows that I've got shares in the company?'

'As far as I'm aware, no-one else.' Sally shrugged. 'Not even John. Mind you, everyone knows there are several anonymous minority shareholders. Why?'

'Oh, I just think it's better if the others don't know, that's all. They might think I've got an ulterior motive in coming back here. OK, I'll admit I was tempted to sell my shares a while back. There must be any number of people in the locality willing to invest in the Mill, but my parents persuaded me to hang on to them. After all, they were a gift from Bryn and Arnold.'

'Thank goodness for that, Annis — if you decided to sell out, I'd feel even more isolated.' The relief on Sally's face was obvious.

Annis looked at her friend sympathetically. There had always been an empathy between the two young women and she felt a pang of guilt for distancing herself for so long.

'I'm so sorry, Sally. I'm afraid I've been so preoccupied with my own problems these past years that I've neglected you.'

'Well, that's understandable, but I have missed you.'

'I've missed you, too,' Annis assured her. 'And you're right. I have been kept up to date with everything, but my father's been dealing with all my financial affairs on my behalf, and to be honest, apart from signing any necessary papers, I just couldn't be bothered with it. Of course, when Bryn was so ill, I suppose he could have confided in someone about the other shareholders.'

'No, he still uses the same financial consultant that he's always had — a trustworthy friend who handled his affairs with complete discretion when Uncle Bryn couldn't do it. I know because there were a few enquiries and absolutely everything had to go past him.'

Annis nodded. 'Well, you'll be pleased to know that you can welcome me back into the fold, Sally.'

Sally sighed as if a weight had been lifted from her shoulders.

'It's going to make life a lot easier for me with you around.'

'Well, don't expect any miracles.' Annis grinned at her friend. 'Now, what's next?'

'Why Didn't You Tell Me?'

The next couple of days passed in a whirl. Heathercote Mill was certainly a thriving concern and it didn't take long for Annis to get back into the swing of things. On Tuesday afternoon, she went to see Bryn Freeman and he arranged for her to move into the staff quarters in the grounds of the Mill the next day.

'Come and see me when you can, Annis,' Bryn said. 'It gets lonely stuck up here all day.'

'Then why don't you come down-stairs and see what's going on?' Annis asked him gently.

'Because I can't get about like I used to and I'd be in the way,' the old gentleman told her with a sigh.

'Nonsense — I'm sure there's lots you could do, and it can't be good for you to be stuck up here all day.'

'You're just as bossy as ever, aren't

you?' He chuckled. 'So what would you have me do, then?'

She thought quickly to come up with something that would appeal to him.

'Would you find it interesting to sit in on one or two of Sally's interviews?'

He ran his fingers through his shock of white hair. 'That's women's stuff — all those flouncy dresses and cakes!' he said defensively.

'What about the wine, the cars and the marquees — to say nothing of the music?'

'I'll think about it,' he promised. 'Now, tell me what you've been up to while you've been away. It's been a long time.'

Annis answered his questions as fully as she felt appropriate, aware that his bright blue eyes never left her face. She told him about her family and their new home in Dorset and her brother, Tim, who was travelling in Indonesia. She told him about her job in London and the flat she shared with a couple of other girls from the office.

When eventually she got up to go, he took hold of her hand.

'Come and see me again soon, lass, and I'll think about what you've said about putting in an appearance down-stairs now and again. It's easy to get into the habit of staying cloistered in the security of one's own four walls.'

* * *

On Wednesday afternoon, Sally's husband, John, returned from his course and greeted Annis with a bear-hug.

'It's wonderful to see you again, Annis. You've left it far too long. Now, what's all this Sally tells me about you insisting on moving into the staff quarters tonight? You didn't have to do that, you know . . . ' He trailed off, catching sight of Tristan beckoning to him. 'No peace for the wicked! I'm afraid we're going to have to catch up later, Annis.'

Annis was very fond of John who was like another brother to her. She watched him now as he spoke with Tristan. John was as thin as a lathe, with sunbleached tousled hair, twinkling blue eyes and boundless energy. Sally had met him when she first began working at the Mill and it had been love at first sight.

Annis packed-up her belongings and moved them from Sally and John's cottage to her room in the staff wing. The room was basic but clean and comfortable, and the view she had of the rolling Kentish countryside from the window was magnificent. Annis took a deep breath. This was what she had missed during the past years. She liked the city, but she was a country girl at heart.

After unpacking her few belongings, she went along to the kitchen where Chef organized some supper on a tray for her.

That night, she slept like a log and awoke next morning feeling refreshed and ready to face any challenges that the day might bring.

Going down to the staff dining-room, she found herself sitting opposite Ross. He glanced up briefly from his breakfast, a slight frown furrowing his forehead.

'So, how come you're gracing us with your presence? I thought you were staying with Sally and John?'

'They haven't got much space, and since John's been away I thought they'd like some time alone.'

Ross took a slice of toast. 'I'm still interested to know why you're helping us out like this.'

'I want to spend some time with Sally. She and I go back a long way and we've got a lot of catching up to do.'

'And are you finding things much changed? Apart from the obvious alterations to the buildings?' He bit into his toast and looked at her, head on one side.

'Actually, I think it's lost something — some of its individuality, perhaps. It's become just another business.'

'Don't tell me you're sentimental,

Miss Fuller? Surely change is an inevitable part of progress?'

'Just so long as it's not change for change's sake. When the wedding business was first starting up, I think our customers valued the personal touch. For instance, we used to give the bride and her bridesmaids a small gift on the wedding day. That seems to have been dispensed with.'

'But you didn't give the amount of discount we do nowadays,' Ross pointed out.

'I can see we're never going to agree.' Annis sighed. 'Everything just seems rather impersonal these days, which is a pity.'

'Yes, well, as I've said, we have to move on. Talking of which, I need to make a move right now.' He got to his feet. 'I've got a meeting in fifteen minutes. Please excuse me.'

Annis watched him as he stopped to speak to Vicki, the attractive young blonde who worked on reception. Vicki laughed at something Ross said and

Annis had an inexplicable feeling of envy at the apparent ease of their relationship.

After breakfast, Annis went for a brisk walk and encountered John who was tidying some flower borders.

'The grounds are looking good, John,' she told him.

'We do our best.' He seemed pleased. 'I've got a good team, but all these courses and meetings that we have to go to are such a nuisance. If only we could be left in peace to get on with the job in hand, then we'd get considerably more done.' He raised his eyebrows suddenly, and then grimaced. 'What on earth does *she* want?'

Annis followed his gaze and saw an attractive dark-haired woman in a green suit making her way across the grass towards them. It was Stella Freeman.

John saw Annis's ashen face.

'You did realise Stella was still around? Sally did tell you?'

Annis's mouth had gone dry and she pulled herself together with difficulty.

'Yes, of course — I just didn't expect to run into her quite so soon, that's all.'

Stella Freeman was in her early thirties, carefully made up, with dark curly hair, expertly styled, and a hard mouth painted glaring red. Her smile did not reach her eyes which were cold and unfriendly, but then, she was probably just as surprised by Annis's presence as Annis was by hers.

'Hello, Annis, I heard you were visiting.' She held out a beautifully manicured hand. 'How are things in the great metropolis?'

'As manic as ever!'

'No change there then. Was it a good course, John?'

'Interesting, I suppose, but I'd rather have been here.' John leaned on his fork. 'There's a lot to be done here and I can't really afford the time to be gallivanting off on courses.'

'Well, I won't keep you then. Actually, I was looking for Tristan — have you seen him this morning?'

'Sorry, no, but if I do, I'll tell him you

want him, shall I?' John turned back to his work. 'Not answering his mobile, I take it?'

'He's left it behind. Typical!' Stella gave a little laugh. 'I suppose you've met my brother, Tristan, haven't you, Annis?'

Annis nodded, wishing the other woman would go away.

'Perhaps you and I could get together sometime over a drink?' Stella plucked a minute piece of fluff from her jacket sleeve. 'How long are you planning to be around?'

Annis hesitated, realising that the older woman was fully aware of her discomfiture. The last thing on earth she wanted to do was to socialise with Stella Freeman.

'Oh, I'm not too sure yet. It rather depends on circumstances. It could be a week or two — perhaps longer.'

Stella's green eyes narrowed and Annis realised she would have to be careful. She certainly didn't want to make an enemy of Andrew's ex-wife.

That wouldn't help matters at all.

Stella shrugged, murmured a good-bye, and headed off in the direction of the conference centre.

John seemed irritated.

'Whenever I look up, that woman seems to be peering over my shoulder! Sorry about all that, Annis.'

'Oh, not to worry. I knew I'd run into her sooner or later,' she said more light-heartedly than she felt.

John looked rather pointedly at his watch and, taking the hint, Annis said a hasty goodbye and hurried over to the office.

'I've just run into Stella,' she told Sally.

Sally bit her lip and carried on with what she was doing for a moment or two. It was as if trying to avoid the subject, thought Annis.

'Sally, is there something else I should know? You mentioned Stella was back in Heronsbridge, but I get the distinct impression there's a bit more to it than that.'

Sally looked anxiously at her friend and mumbled, 'Yes, well, I — er — I told you that she lives in the village now, but I should also have said that she's been working here part-time since last October.'

Annis sank down on the nearest chair. 'Why on earth didn't you tell me? Do you honestly think that I'd have come here if I'd known both Stella and her brother were working here?'

'That's exactly why I didn't tell you, Annis.' Sally stopped what she was doing. 'Can't you see how difficult all this is for me? You're my closest friend and I don't want to see you get hurt all over again, but life has to move on and — well, Stella felt she needed to do something, so Uncle Bryn agreed to her working here.'

There was silence while Annis tried to calm her breathing.

'I see. Well, I knew there were changes around here, but I'd no idea how many,' she said slowly. 'Hasn't it occurred to you that if anyone's trying to make problems for you, it could well be Stella? After all, she's pretty unscrupulous, if the past is anything to go by.'

'Annis, I'm sorry. I can see that I ought to have told you about Stella sooner, but believe me, she's efficient at her job and we get on tolerably well. She does manage to rub John up the wrong way, and you know how good-natured he is as a rule,' Sally admitted, 'but no, I honestly don't believe she's at the root of my problems.'

Annis shrugged; her friend always wanted to believe the best of people, but she had never been a particularly good judge of character.

'And what exactly is Stella's job?'

'She's personal assistant to Ross,' Sally said miserably.

Annis tried hard to keep control because she realised that Sally was in a difficult position — torn between loyalty to Bryn and the business and herself. She swallowed hard.

'You realise this puts an entirely different complexion on things? I'm not at all sure if I can remain here now, much as I'd like to help you out. I thought long and hard about coming here in the first place, as you well know, and now that I have, I think it was probably a big mistake. You really ought to have told me about Stella. It's awkward for both of us, not just me.'

'Yes, I can see that now.' Sally looked uncomfortable. 'Look, I'm sure you won't run into her too often. I realise all this must bring back a lot of bad memories. Stella's been away for a few days and I thought you'd have enough to cope with for the present, just being here. But please don't run away, Annis,' she said desperately. 'I need you, and Uncle Bryn does too. Stay around for a few days, for his sake, if not for mine.'

'OK, I'll stay until the end of the week and then I'll review things. I can see the predicament you're in, Sally, and I really do want to help, but it's difficult.'

It was now crystal clear to Annis why Ross resented her presence so much. He obviously wanted to protect Stella as well as Bryn.

'Stella asked me to have a drink with her,' she told Sally. 'Can you believe that?'

'Well, there you are then — she's obviously offering you an olive branch.'

Annis stared at her friend in disbelief.

'You just don't get it, do you, Sally? I've tried to move on, but now I'm actually here, it's as if I'm back where I started five years ago, on the day that I learned that Andrew wasn't in love with me after all! But at least then he was still alive . . . ' she added bitterly.

'I feel dreadfully guilty.' Sally was visibly upset. 'I should never have asked you to come here. I knew it would be hard, but I hadn't realised quite how much . . . '

Sally broke off as the internal phone rang. It was reception, with a message to say that her latest clients had arrived.

While Sally went to fetch them,

Annis poured herself a glass of water and tried to pull herself together. If she went to pieces it wouldn't help anyone. She had run away from this place once before, but now she was back and she didn't intend to let Stella, Ross or Tristan drive her away again — at least, not until she'd had a chance to suss out what, if anything, was going on at Heathercote Mill that might put Sally out of a job.

* * *

After a busy morning, Annis was sorting out a pile of invoices and contemplating lunch when Tristan came into the office.

'Ah, here you are!' he said. 'I was wondering if you're ready for something to eat?'

She carried on with what she was doing. 'I'll ring through for some sandwiches in a minute.'

He moved some papers and sat on the desk.

'Actually, I thought you might fancy going out for some lunch, to somewhere away from this place. Come on, you've been on the go all week. Where's Sally, by the way?' He asked her casually, but she sensed he was trying to catch Sally out.

'She's with Mr Freeman. She wanted to discuss a new idea with him.

Annis looked up just in time to see a slight frown flicker across Tristan's face.

'What new idea?' he asked.

She shrugged. 'You'll have to ask Sally, and yes, I would like to go out for lunch, please.'

She scribbled a note for Sally, popped the invoices that she'd been working on into a drawer, and fetched her jacket. She knew exactly what Sally was discussing with Bryn, but she had no intention of telling Tristan.

Sally and Annis had an idea which they wanted to discuss with Madame Cecile that afternoon, but first Sally needed to OK it with Bryn.

Tristan took Annis to The Royal Oak

in Heronsbridge where they ordered chicken and chips in a basket. Tristan was much more down to earth than Ross, and Annis found him good company. He kept her amused with a series of anecdotes about some of the conferences.

'So when did you come to work at the Mill?' Annis asked him casually.

'Soon after my grandfather died.'

'Oh, yes, of course — it was a pity you didn't get to meet your Uncle Arnold while he was alive. He was a great character.'

'So everyone keeps telling me, but he and my father didn't hit it off.'

Prudently Annis changed the subject.

'So you and Ross manage the conference centre between you? How do you find that works?'

'I take it that's a tactful way of asking how we get on?' Tristan laughed. 'Well, we muddle along together — we beg to differ on a number of issues, but then, it takes all sorts. How about you? Why are you so keen to be here after all this time?'

'I've told you before, I haven't seen Sally, John or Bryn for a while, for one, and feel I need a change of direction. Sally needs a helping hand and we get on well together.'

'So what do you make of it all?' Tristan looked at her keenly.

Annis deliberately misunderstood him.

'I like the new units, but I find the whole enterprise more impersonal than it used to be, which is a pity.'

'Actually I meant what do you make of all the problems that the wedding side of the business keeps having? After all, I suspect that's why Sally really asked you down here, isn't it?'

'I've only been here for a very short time so who am I to comment?'

'Oh, come on, I'm sure you've noticed the mistakes too?'

Annis paused. 'One or two, yes,' she said at last, 'but surely that's inevitable because of the way you both expect Sally to work?'

He laid down his knife and fork, his eyes glinting. 'Go on . . . '

'Well, she's constantly having to deal with interruptions from various quarters, and she's often called away to different parts of the building to attend meetings. She loses continuity, she can't help it.'

'Yes, I see,' said Tristan. 'So what would you suggest to make things easier for her?'

'Well, it seems to me that Sally isn't given a chance to concentrate on the wedding business. She should be allowed to get on with her work without so many disturbances.' She had a sudden inspiration. 'Perhaps she could do with a break from Heathercote Mill altogether. She works so hard. Aren't there any courses she could go on? That might help.'

Tristan looked thoughtful.

'It's a coincidence but, as it happens, there's one next week. I'm booked on it, but if Sally agreed, then I'm sure I could arrange for her to go in my place. That's if you're prepared to stay and cover for her, of course.'

He wasn't to know that Sally had already mentioned the course rather wistfully to Annis, and had said that she hadn't been given the opportunity to go on it.

'That sounds like a good idea,' Annis said. 'And of course I'll stay.'

As they left the pub, Tristan took Annis's arm in a friendly manner and, in spite of his relationship to Stella, she found herself warming to him.

* * *

To Annis's relief, Sally was delighted at the prospect of going away on the course.

'I've no idea how you managed it, Annis. You've obviously used your charm on Tristan. It'll be wonderful to have a few days away from this place and to know that the business has been left in safe hands. Thank you so much for persuading Tristan to let me go.'

'It wasn't difficult — he came up with the idea himself after I'd put it into his head.' Annis laughed. 'Anyway, you've as much right as anyone else to go on a course. You're letting the others trample all over you. You need to be more assertive.'

'I know, but it's difficult . . . If only you'd come to work here on a permanent basis again, then perhaps we could get things back on an even keel and I'd do things differently.'

Bryn had given the go-ahead for the idea that Sally had consulted him about that morning, and so, presently, the two girls went along to the boutique to see Madame Cecile.

'Hats,' Madame Cecile mused. 'You know, that's a very good idea. After all, it can be quite difficult to find the exact hat to match an outfit There's no reason why we shouldn't give it a try — in a small way, to begin with. We already hire out top hats for gentlemen.'

Madame Cecile was obviously enthusiastic, and Sally and Annis exchanged delighted glances.

'Of course, I'm far too busy with the

dressmaking to get too involved with millinery as a sideline,' she told them, 'but in a few years' time when my daughter, Camille, is fully trained, that might be an area she would like to specialise in. It would also be a good use for the empty unit next door, because we don't have the storage space here.'

'I've met your daughter, Madame,' Annis told her. 'She's quite charming.'

Madame Cecile glowed with pride.

The three women discussed hats for a little while and then stopped to admire the gown that Madame was working on. It was in oyster-coloured satin with a scooped neckline. Madame was in the process of adding the finishing touches, a trail of silver embroidery with the merest suggestion of peach here and there.

'It's one of your loveliest creations yet,' Sally complimented her. 'What about the veil?'

Madame smiled and her entire face was transformed, so that Annis could see that she was much younger than she had at first thought.

'The veil is to be made from antique lace — a family heirloom, apparently. I'll show you the sketch. Camille designed it. She's so artistic!'

Annis and Sally stayed to have coffee with Madame Cecile and Lara. Lara served it in minute bone china cups with thin almond biscuits, and Annis observed that while Lara rarely added anything to the conversation, she took in everything that was being said, her dark eyes darting constantly from one person to another.

Presently the girls made their way back to the office.

'Well, that went better than I expected,' Sally said. 'Madame Cecile has been known to oppose new ideas in the past. What did you make of Lara?'

'She didn't have much to say for herself, did she? And she seems kind of miserable. Perhaps she doesn't enjoy her work.'

'You've summed her up pretty well.

Actually, I don't really know much about her. She only works part-time. Her husband runs that antiques shop in the village.'

'Really? Then I've met him — it was when I went into Heronsbridge the day I arrived. He seems a surly sort of individual,' she remarked.

'Yes, I think he probably is,' agreed Sally. 'But I wonder what Tristan was doing there? Maybe he'd just dropped in to see Vicki. You'll have met Vicki — the blonde girl who works here in reception — very attractive. She's Lara's older daughter.'

'Vicki is?' Annis was frankly amazed. 'Well, it just goes to show!'

'Actually, it was Vicki's younger sister who came to work here for a short while after Zoe left, but it just didn't work out . . . She's not a bit like Vicki.'

'You said she wasn't suited to the job — so what happened?'

'Well, I usually get on with most people, wouldn't you say?' Annis nodded, intrigued. 'Well, Kelly just didn't fit in. In the beginning she seemed fine, but after a short while she seemed to lose interest — in fact, to be honest, she was extremely uncooperative and used to criticise everything that I did. Sometimes she was downright rude.'

'Wow!' Annis stared at her friend. 'If she rubbed you up the wrong way then she must have been difficult! You've always been such an easy person to work with.'

'Thanks for that vote of confidence,' Sally grinned. 'But I'm not sure if everyone around here would agree with you.'

'Then they must be the awkward ones. So, I suppose you had no alternative but to fire Kelly?'

'It didn't actually come to that. One day she told me she wasn't coming back because it wasn't working out for her either. I asked her if she'd be interested in having another job at the Mill — I won't repeat what she said to that!'

‘Poor you,’ Annis sympathised. ‘It sounds as if it was all rather unpleasant.’

‘It’s certainly an episode I’d rather draw a line under. I suspect that’s why Lara doesn’t say much when I go over to the boutique.’

‘Surely she doesn’t hold it against you?’

‘Who can say? She’s never mentioned the subject.’

Sally waved to John who was busy in the distance.

‘Well, let’s see what’s next on the agenda for today.’

Another Muddle

It was a beautiful evening and Annis decided to take a walk in the grounds before going up to her room. She strolled down to the lake and sat on one of the benches, watching the water fowl. The shadows were deepening, and as she looked across the water she suddenly made out several life-like shapes on the opposite shore. They looked like statues and she was surprised that she hadn't noticed them before. She resolved to ask Sally about them in the morning. They had an ethereal quality about them, blending in with the greenery.

Suddenly, though, as she watched, they began to move. She blinked in disbelief, but there was no doubt about it — they were weaving to and fro. Next second, she distinctly heard the sound of distant music.

She jumped at the sound of a deep chuckle behind her. Spinning round, she saw Ross Hadley laughing down at her.

'Your face is an absolute picture! They're quite real — you're not dreaming, I can assure you.'

'Who are they?' she breathed.

'Members of a local youth theatre and dance group, rehearsing for 'A Midsummer Night's Dream' — a modern open-air version. They hadn't anywhere to put on the show, partly because they're working on a shoe-string, so when Bryn heard about them he said they could come here.'

He sat down beside her on the bench. 'They have to rehearse as and when it fits in with our schedule, of course, and it's on the strict understanding that they don't interfere with other activities. Madame Cecile's daughter, Millie, is in the group and so is her boyfriend — he's a waiter here for the summer.'

'How will the play fit in around all

the weddings that are due to take place?'

'Ah, the actual performances are going to be over the bank holiday weekend. The Friday evening's free for the dress rehearsal and then there's Sunday afternoon and Monday evening. Bryn's all for supporting the young folk. It's given him an added interest.'

'That's good,' she said approvingly.

They sat for a while longer watching the players.

'Have you seen the staff garden yet?' Ross asked her. 'John's making a superb job of it.'

She shook her head. 'Not properly. I've only caught glimpses of it from Bryn's flat.'

'Come on — I'll show you.'

She followed Ross across the grass and through the archway leading to the rear of the Mill. He unlocked a gate in the wall, and as she went through, Annis gasped in surprise.

'It's amazing! When I worked here

before, this was a vegetable garden.'

'The kitchen garden's through there now,' he said, indicating another gate. 'This new part of the garden is for all the staff, but it's mostly for Bryn's benefit. On a sunny day he can sit out here when he feels like it.'

The garden was charming. Brick paths meandered here and there between an abundance of flowering shrubs, and there was a small lawn with an attractive water feature. Roses scrambled up a pergola and a wonderful perfume of honeysuckle and nicotiana filled the evening air.

Ross also took her to see the new, neatly laid-out kitchen garden and the recently restored tennis courts which had been in a poor condition when Annis had been there last.

Peaches still clung to the garden walls, however, and she shook her head, trying to shake off the sudden memory of Andrew picking them for her. Even now she could see his laughing face.

'It'll get better, trust me — time heals,' Ross said, in a surprisingly gentle tone.

'Does it?' she asked bitterly. 'I haven't noticed.'

For a while, they sat there in companionable silence beneath an arbour of roses, then Ross's mobile phone rang and, after a brief conversation, he got to his feet.

'I'm sorry — duty calls. One of the bar staff hasn't turned up. No-one else is available, so I'll have to lend a hand.'

'You will?' She gaped at him.

'Yes, is that so surprising? I'm quite a dab hand with a cocktail shaker. I always knew my student days working as a barman would pay off. D'you fancy a nightcap?'

She shook her head. 'I think I'll just sit here a bit longer — it's so soothing. But thanks, Ross. The garden's great and I'll be sure to tell John what a wonderful job he's done here.'

'He'll appreciate that. I'll wish you goodnight then.'

She sat in the garden, deep in her thoughts, for a while longer. It was a tranquil spot and the scent from the roses was intoxicating. Ross had proved a pleasant companion and she realised she'd seen a more sympathetic side to him that evening.

Presently, she heard the sound of voices and muffled laughter from the other side of the wall. Annis assumed that some of the younger members of staff were taking a stroll around the garden.

Eventually she decided to return to her room because it was getting chilly, but when she reached the gate she found that it had been locked. Muttering in irritation, she rummaged in her bag for her mobile, but it wasn't there and she realised she'd left it in her room. She had no choice but to trail back along the paths to look for another way out.

To her relief, she encountered two figures from the play, still dressed in their eerie green costumes, and looking as startled as she must have done. It took her a moment or two to realise it was Millie and Dean.

'Can you tell me how to get out of the garden? I don't have a key and someone's locked the gate.'

They looked a bit sheepish. 'Well, actually we don't have a key either. We — er — nipped over the wall. I climbed on to Dean's shoulders and . . . '

Annis laughed. 'I get the general idea. Well, if you managed to climb in here, you must have some way to get out again?'

'There are a few crates behind the shed,' Dean explained.

After a few moments the three of them landed on the other side of the wall, dusted themselves down and strolled back in the direction of the main entrance.

'Thanks, guys — and I won't tell if you don't,' Annis promised, giving them a conspiratorial wink. 'By the way, I'm looking forward to the production of 'The Dream'. It must be a lot of hard work.'

Millie nodded. 'It is, but it's great fun. To be honest, acting is what I want to do, but my mother wants me to do an Art and Design course — she says there's no future in the theatre.'

'I expect she's just concerned that you won't get a secure job,' Annis told her. 'You know, you could always compromise . . . '

'How do you mean?' Millie asked, dark eyes alight with interest.

'Lots of people do more than one degree nowadays. Why don't you go for the Art and Design course but carry on with dance and theatre as a hobby. And then . . . '

'But it'd take for ever, and once I was qualified my mother would expect me to come back here and work with her. I'd never have any space to do my own thing,' Millie protested.

'Sometimes doing your own thing doesn't work out quite how you'd expect it to,' Annis said softly. 'Have you tried talking to your mother — telling her exactly how you feel about things?'

Dean took Millie's hand.

'She won't listen!' he said. 'She just won't believe that Millie doesn't want to join her in the boutique. She thinks I'm a bad influence on you, doesn't she, Millie?'

'My mother loves her work, Miss Fuller, and can't understand why I want to do something so completely different,' Millie said with a sigh. 'She thinks my love for the theatre is just a passing phase.'

Annis sympathised with the girl, but she knew she couldn't interfere too much. Millie was going to have to learn to stand up to her mother, who seemed very domineering.

The two young people linked arms and Annis parted company with them at the entrance to the Mill.

* * *

The following day was hectic from start to finish. There was a conference taking place which wound up at lunchtime and then it was all hands on deck to get everything ready for a big society wedding, due to take place the following day. The bride, Megan Smythe, was the daughter of an influential local businessman who had a bevy of daughters, and Megan was the first of them to marry.

This time it was the bride's father who was determined to make his presence felt. In the run up to the wedding, Mr Smythe had been on the phone countless times to check the arrangements, and had turned up unexpectedly on several occasions. Now, the day before the wedding, here he was in the office yet again.

He was a big man and seemed to fill the room.

'I want to see the chef, to go over the catering arrangements.'

'Everything's in hand, Mr Smythe,' Sally told him reassuringly. 'They're very busy in the kitchen at the moment because a conference party has only just left, but I can assure you that Chef and his team have everything under control for tomorrow.'

At Mr Smythe's insistence, Sally rang through to see if Luis could be persuaded to leave his kitchen to talk to him but, as she had anticipated, Luis refused point blank. He did, however, concede to speak to Mr Smythe for a minute or two on the phone. It was a compromise that Mr Smythe had to be content with.

Then Mr Smythe decided that he needed to inspect the marquee that had been assembled that morning, and immediately found fault with the arrangement of the tables, even though he himself had approved the seating plan.

By the time he had gone, Sally was a nervous wreck. Annis poured her a coffee and made her sit down for a few moments.

After that, everything else seemed to go swimmingly until Sally contacted the bakers and discovered a problem with the cake.

She came off the phone ashen-faced.

'It's happened again!'

'What has? Whatever's the matter, Sally?'

Sally was looking in her book. 'The cake should be three tiers — two fruit and one sponge. That's what I ordered. But the bakers have made two tiers — one fruit and one chocolate!'

'Let's look.' Annis checked the records on the computer and frowned. 'Yes, the notes on here are the same as in your book. And I double-checked the entry at the beginning of the week, so it's got to be the baker's mistake.'

Sally looked as if she were ready to weep. 'No, they say we changed the order from the original a few weeks ago — but I don't have any recollection of doing so at all.'

Annis was as puzzled as Sally, but she tried to think sensibly.

'Look, it's no good wasting time speculating as to how it happened. We've got to try to put it right. Is it the same baker that we used to use — Sam Wallis?'

'Yes, but it'll be too late to do anything at this stage.' Sally blew her nose. 'Sam's always so reliable, and I only phoned him to check on delivery times because Mr Smythe wants the cake here an hour earlier than previously arranged. Otherwise I wouldn't have discovered the mistake until the cake actually arrived! Whatever are we going to do?'

'Don't despair — just you get on with whatever else needs doing. I'm going to see if I can sort this out with Sam right now. No-one will miss me.'

Annis rummaged in her bag and produced a bus timetable.

'I knew this would come in handy — if I hurry, I'll be able to catch the bus. Expect me when you see me, Sal!' She snatched up her jacket, ran down the drive, and was just in time for the hourly bus.

At any other time, Annis would have enjoyed the bus trip along leafy sun-dappled lanes, but she was far too preoccupied. If Sally's suspicion that someone was deliberately setting out to cause problems for her was confirmed, then Annis would need to confront Ross and Tristan.

* * *

The baker's shop was in the middle of a village that was four miles from Heronsbridge. Baker Sam Wallis was both delighted and astonished to see Annis again after so many years.

She came straight to the point, explaining their predicament.

Sam rubbed his chin thoughtfully. 'I know folk change their mind, but it does make it difficult if it's at the last minute like this, especially as the order's already been changed once. It shouldn't be too hard to sort this one out, mind you, but I wouldn't do it for everyone.'

He leaned on the counter and thumbed through his order book.

'It just so happens that I'm ahead of myself with the orders and there's another round fruit cake the right size, all marzipanned ready for another wedding. I can easily decorate that. And I've got a sponge cake iced ready for a wedding anniversary. I can easily adapt that and no-one will be any the wiser. Yes, if I set to directly I can have the whole thing ready for delivery tomorrow morning, as arranged. I might need to add on a bit to the cost, mark you, but only if I can't sell the chocolate one. Now, have a cup of tea and I'll run you back to Heronsbridge in the delivery van. I've got another cake to deliver over there for a twenty-first birthday.'

'Who rang you up to change the order the first time, Sam?' Annis asked.

Sam screwed up his round face in concentration. 'Blowed if I can remember. Hang on, I'll have a word with the missus.'

Beryl Wallis helped out in the shop from time to time and dealt with any business calls. She distinctly remembered a woman ringing up to change the original order a few weeks back. Unfortunately, she didn't know who the woman had been, but what she did know — was absolutely certain about — was that it hadn't been Sally.

Annis was surprised to discover that she felt relieved. Not for one minute had she thought it had been Sally, but now it seemed that it couldn't have been Ross or Tristan, either.

* * *

By the time Sam dropped Annis off in the village, she was feeling a lot happier. Sally's suspicions were confirmed. It wasn't Sally herself who'd been making all the mistakes. Someone was deliberately trying to make trouble — either for Sally herself or for 'Something Borrowed, Something Blue'.

Annis took her time going back to the Mill, strolling through the village deep in thought, pausing to look into the window of the post office-cum-gift shop. She jumped when she was tapped on the shoulder and found Tristan laughing at her.

'Sorry! I didn't mean to startle you! Where are you off to?'

'I'm just making my way back to the Mill after a walk,' she told him, carefully avoiding any mention of her visit to the baker's.

He fell into step beside her.

'All set for tomorrow's wedding?'

'Yes. Everything's on target.'

'Good. Mr Smythe is an important customer.'

'So I believe.' She felt inexplicably annoyed. 'Although, actually, I think all the customers are equally important.'

'Too right,' he agreed hastily. 'Are you happy about taking over from Sally next week?'

'Of course. Why wouldn't I be?' she said, a little snappily.

'No reason — just asking. Remember to shout if you need any help. By the way, Bryn has asked you, me and Ross to join him for dinner this evening, so that we can discuss what's happening during the next couple of weeks — forward planning, you know.'

'Tonight?' Annis was taken aback. 'But we're pretty tied up with tomorrow's wedding.'

Tristan tucked his arm into hers as they crossed the road and began to walk along the lane that led towards the Mill.

'Chill out. It'll only be for an hour or so. Bryn is anxious for you to be there, but Sally's excused on this occasion.'

'But she's not going off until Wednesday. Won't she need to know what's happening, too?'

'Not really. On Monday she'll just be seeing potential clients as usual, and then she's got Tuesday afternoon off.'

'Right,' Annis said. 'Well, I suppose it would be a good idea for me to have an overview of what's going on.'

Annis wasn't happy about the arrangement but realised she'd have to go along with it.

'Stella seems to be keeping well,' she said, as they approached the Mill.

'Yes, she is, but it took a long time. Did you two actually meet when you were here before?'

'Of course. I saw her on several occasions before — before I realised she was involved with Andrew.'

'And yet I gather you've never met Ross before now?'

Annis shook her head. 'He went back up north after — after the party.'

'You must hate him for bringing Stella back here and introducing her to Andrew.'

'Hate is too strong a word, Tristan. I can hardly hold Ross responsible for what happened, can I?' And as she uttered the words, she was aware that she really meant them. It was hardly Ross's fault that Stella and Andrew had fallen in love.

'No, I suppose it could be said that Ross had as much reason to feel angry with Andrew as you did. After all, there was a time when he and Stella . . . '

Annis stared at him. 'You know, I hadn't thought about it quite like that.

We're both the victims of circumstance, aren't we?'

'I suppose if you think about it, so am I.' Tristan grinned. 'Whoever would have thought I'd settle down in a place like this? Oh, well, back to the grind again. I had to do a quick hop to the post office for Vicki on reception. They've run out of stamps.'

Sally looked up as Annis entered the office.

'You've been a long time. How did it go?'

Annis told her about what had happened at the baker's and also mentioned the dinner with Bryn.

'Oh, good, you've been told about it,' said Sally. 'Uncle Bryn usually has these meetings once a fortnight, but not usually on a Friday. Anyway, I've pleaded to be let off — I can't spare the time. But you need to be there, so John's going to help me out here.'

Sally passed a hand wearily across her forehead.

'Annis, I don't know what I'd have

done without you this afternoon. I know we need to get to the bottom of what's been going on, but at least the cake's sorted out for tomorrow. It's been absolute pandemonium here! You'll never believe what's happened now!'

Annis could not believe that anything else could have gone wrong in her absence and listened as her friend told her about the latest drama.

'We've had the bride-to-be in here, practically hysterical — one of the bridesmaids has gone down with chicken pox, would you believe! Anyway, poor Megan couldn't find any one else to take her place at such short notice, but it just so happened that Ross was here and he came up with a stroke of genius, bless him. He suggested that Millie might stand in. She's a bit older than the cousin who's ill, but she's small for her age and dark-haired. Fortunately, Millie agreed and Madame Cecile is making the alterations to the dress as we speak.'

To Sally's amazement, Annis began to laugh helplessly.

'I can't imagine what you find so funny,' said Sally reproachfully.

'Well,' said Annis, still giggling, 'I know we offer a complete package, but I didn't realise that included providing bridesmaids as well — let's hope it's not a substitute bride or groom the next time round!'

* * *

That evening, Annis found herself in the company of both Ross and Tristan at the same time, and had the rare opportunity to study them together. She decided that the two men were quite different, not just in looks, but in personality, too.

'So you're in charge of 'Something Borrowed, Something Blue' while Sally's away next week, eh, Annis?' said Bryn. 'You've no idea what it means to me to see you back here again. Sally deserves a break too. She's been working herself into the ground.'

'I'm not sure that going on a course

for four days can be termed a break — although it'll certainly be a change,' Annis told him.

Bryn poured more wine.

'This wedding tomorrow — I think I'll be around to keep an eye on things. Ray Smythe's father, Arthur, was a friend of Arnold's and comes to play chess with me now and again. I know the family quite well.'

'Yes, well, everything's nicely under control, so it's just a question of the bride and groom turning up at the church,' Annis said, tongue in cheek.

Bryn chuckled. 'Yes, Ross has already told me about the near catastrophe over the bridesmaid. What a blessing that young Millie's agreed to step in. She's a lovely young lass. Anyway, let's toast the happy couple, and then we'll run through the schedule for next week.'

* * *

The following morning, Annis awoke to a grey drizzle, but by twelve o'clock, when the wedding party was due to arrive from the church, the sky had cleared and a watery sun had broken through.

The reception surpassed all expectations and the cake was a triumph.

Afterwards, a beaming Mr and Mrs Smythe came to thank Sally personally, and to issue an invitation for the staff to join the celebrations that evening.

Annis was pleased to see Sally smiling and looking more relaxed.

'For the first time in weeks, I feel confident — thanks to you, Annis. I'm even beginning to enjoy myself,' Sally told her.

'Well, if anything goes wrong next week, it'll be down to me,' Annis replied, as she and Sally went their separate ways to get ready for the evening celebrations.

Once they'd changed, they went — along with the rest of staff — to join the wedding party in the marquee.

Ross and Tristan looked very elegant in dinner jackets and bow ties.

Bryn, still a distinguished-looking man, was deep in conversation with Arthur Smythe, but he interrupted his conversation to introduce Annis, Sally and John to Arthur Smythe and to the wedding party.

Annis was glad that she'd packed a couple of evening dresses. The one she was wearing that evening was sea-green with shoestring straps, and showed off her slender figure to its best advantage.

She obligingly danced with John and one or two other members of staff before finding her way to the table allocated to them.

Vicki was already there, sitting between Tristan and a young man who also worked on reception.

Millie — looking an absolute picture in her pale-pink bridesmaid's dress — came over to chat, accompanied by two of the smallest bridesmaids who were obviously sisters, angelic-looking little girls with golden hair.

'Two little flower girls — Poppy and Daisy,' she said, by way of introduction, and the little girls giggled.

'Are you enjoying yourself, Millie?' enquired Ross.

'Yes, it's been fun — mind you, it's hard work trying to keep up with these two. I've volunteered to look after them for a bit, since Dean's had to go off to sort out some more vegetarian food for the buffet.'

Tristan frowned. 'Has there been a problem with the catering, Sally?'

'No, of course not. There's plenty of food to go round, but the guests like to sample everything, which means the vegetarians sometimes miss out. There's no simple solution.'

The smallest child suddenly wrestled free from Millie.

'Oops, here we go again,' Millie said. 'I think we need a crèche for the tinies!' She shot off in pursuit of the little girl.

Ross exchanged looks with Sally.

'Out of the mouths of babes! There's an idea for you, Sally — a crèche to keep the tinies happy on these occasions.'

'Are you volunteering?' Sally laughed. 'Personally I think guests like to see the little ones, but I suppose they can sometimes get a bit over-excited and fractious by this time of night.'

'It's an idea worth considering,' said Tristan, before turning to Vicki and asking her to dance.

Presently, the little girls' mother rescued Millie, leaving her free to dance with Dean, who had rejoined the staff table and was looking a bit lost.

They whirled away, and Tristan returned to the table with Vicki, just as Stella arrived, wearing a striking red dress.

Ross immediately led Stella on to the dance floor.

Annis watched Ross as he danced with Stella. From a distance, he bore a striking resemblance to Andrew, and for a few moments she was lost in her memories, remembering a similar happy occasion when she and Andrew had danced the night away. She found herself wondering if dancing with Ross would be different and suspected that it would. He was more serious, but he was also more mature and she had the sudden feeling that she would feel safe in his arms.

She thought about what Tristan had said the previous day. Obviously, Stella had been friends with Ross for a long time before she'd fallen for Andrew.

Lost in her thoughts, Annis started when she realised that Ross was speaking to her.

'I came over with the intention of asking you to dance, but if you'd rather not . . . '

As he turned to walk away, Annis caught his sleeve.

'No, please . . . I would like to dance. Thank you, Ross.' She got to her feet and he whirled her away.

Annis soon realised that dancing with Ross wasn't a bit like dancing with Andrew, who had tended to make up the steps as he went along.

Andrew had been such an extrovert and she had loved him for it, but Ross was a competent dancer and she felt strangely secure in his arms.

She knew that he was only dancing with her out of a sense of obligation, but she was grateful to him for the gesture. She could have wished, however, that she didn't feel quite so disturbed by the torrent of feelings raging within her and she was glad when they returned to the table and he asked Sally for the next dance.

Tristan had rejoined their party and was talking to John. Setting down his glass, he held out his hand to Annis. She couldn't very well refuse and accompanied him back on to the floor.

He was not content with one dance, however, and after two, she begged to be excused. He was a bit of a show-off — a clever performer who kept up a constant patter of talk and seemed tireless. Annis wasn't sure if he was trying to impress her or Vicki, who was dancing with one of the wedding guests.

'I could do with some fresh air,'

Annis told him presently, hoping to excuse herself so that she could slip away quietly but, for an answer, Tristan took her by the arm and guided her out of the marquee.

* * *

It was a beautiful, balmy evening and quite a number of guests were strolling towards the lake, but Tristan steered Annis in the opposite direction, towards the Mill. They reached the formal garden and, as they wandered beneath the trees, he suddenly caught her in his arms and kissed her full on the mouth.

He had taken her unawares, and as she came to her senses and pulled away from him, Ross happened to walk past, escorting Bryn back to the Mill. Tristan called out a cheerful goodnight.

'That'll give him something to think about,' he told her, and Annis found herself wishing it had been anyone but Ross who had come along at that moment. Her cheeks flamed.

‘I’d like to go back to the others now, Tristan.’

‘You were the one who wanted to come for a walk. Having second thoughts?’

She realised that she had annoyed him.

‘It was getting hot in the marquee, but now I’m beginning to feel chilly . . . I think you’ve misinterpreted things.’

He laughed. ‘You’re a little tease, aren’t you, Annis Fuller? Either that or you’re playing some kind of game that I haven’t quite fathomed out. Anyway, I’ve had enough of weddings for tonight. I’ll see you around. Sweet dreams!’ And he strode off in the direction of the Mill.

Annis was grateful that no-one could see the colour in her cheeks. She realised just how careful she would have to be around Tristan in future.

Forgetful of the chill in the air, she wandered down to the lake and sat on one of the seats, staring unseeingly into the water.

A short while later Ross came to join her.

‘Has Tristan deserted you?’

‘He had one or two things to do.’

‘Just a friendly word of advice, Annis . . . ’ His eyes narrowed. ‘Tristan came here with Vicki this evening. I’m afraid he’s a bit of a playboy.’

‘Really?’ She got to her feet and met his gaze levelly. ‘Well, I’m quite capable of taking care of myself and making my own judgements, thank you very much. I came outside to get some fresh air, but I’ve had enough now, so I’m going back in.’ And she marched off towards the marquee without looking back. Had she done so, she would have seen Ross staring after her, a curious expression on his face.

Annis was aware that Ross had made her feel cheap for allowing Tristan to flirt with her, and wondered why his opinion of her should matter so much. She sighed, wishing life wasn’t so complicated. Not for the first time, she wondered if she’d made a very big mistake in returning to Heronsbridge.

Getting To Know Ross

On Sunday, Annis firmly refused Sally and John's invitation to lunch, feeling that they needed some time together before Sally went away on her course the following Wednesday.

Instead, she had her meal in the staff dining-room, hoping to renew her acquaintance with former colleagues. In this she was disappointed, because most of the familiar faces from when she'd worked at the hotel previously had gone. She did still know a few members of staff, but none of them were around.

She was just about to go to a solitary window seat when she found herself being hailed by Millie and Dean, who were sitting with a group of friends on the other side of the room.

She was immediately swept up in a round of introductions.

'Mr Freeman's given us permission

to rehearse here this afternoon and he said we could all have our lunch first,' Millie explained. 'We thought of asking him to the rehearsal, but Mr Hadley said he's not to be disturbed because he's worn out from all the excitement of the wedding yesterday.'

'I think he might prefer to see the actual performance, don't you?' Annis said diplomatically, realising that Bryn probably had an afternoon nap these days. 'I tell you what, though: I could come and watch for an hour or so, if you like, so that I can tell him all about it.'

'Would you really?' Millie's face lit up. 'That would be great. We need an audience.'

The youngsters chattered animatedly, like a flock of starlings, and Annis realised that a few years back she had been like that. Full of enthusiasm and vitality.

They were a friendly bunch, and when they'd all finished lunch, she accompanied them down to the lake and sat on the grassy bank, watching them with genuine admiration.

It was a clever interpretation of 'The Dream', and she soon realised that Millie and Dean were by far the most talented. Their performance was inspired, and Millie's dance was so beautiful that it brought tears to Annis's eyes.

The time passed quickly and it was well over an hour and a half later that Millie came over and sat beside Annis on the bank.

'So what did you think, Miss Fuller?'

'I think that you're all very talented and that you should all be very proud of yourselves. I loved your dance, and everything else is coming together beautifully. By the time you've polished up the few areas that your producer's mentioned, it should be superb.'

'Thanks!' Millie beamed at her. 'You can see now why I really want to go into the performing arts in a big way. Oh, I like Art and Design well enough, but I don't want to make a career of it.'

'It's good to have ambition, Millie,'

Annis told her, choosing her words carefully because she didn't want to influence the girl in any way. 'But as I said the other day, it's not a bad idea to have more than one string to your bow.'

Millie smiled wryly, picking a daisy and twirling it round in her fingers. 'I've thought about what you said the other day, Miss Fuller, and I know it makes sense, but my mother works so hard and I want more out of life than that. Besides, Dean and I — well, we're really good together and — well, who knows . . . maybe in a few years time . . . ?'

'So what does your mother think of Dean?' Annis asked.

'Oh, she likes him well enough, but she doesn't realise how serious we are about each other. She thinks I'm still a child; she won't accept that I'm nearly eighteen — that I'm an adult with my own life to lead.'

'Might I offer just one more piece of advice?' Annis smiled. 'Don't do anything on impulse. Think it through first, or you might live to regret it.'

Millie nodded. 'It's strange, but I find it much easier to talk to you and Uncle Bryn than my own mother. Much as I love her, we're not on the same wavelength most of the time. I'm not even sure if I can persuade her to come to the production of 'The Dream'.'

'Oh, I'm sure she wouldn't miss it for the world.' Annis got to her feet and brushed the grass off her skirt. 'Now, I'm going up to see Bryn. Good luck with the rest of the rehearsal and thanks for letting me watch.'

* * *

Bryn looked up with a smile as Annis entered the room.

'Come to cheer me up? Sit down, lass.'

Annis sat on the chair that he'd indicated. 'Do you fancy a game of draughts, or perhaps cards?' she asked, and he chuckled.

'I know you can't abide cards, Annis,

so don't humour me! No, I'd just like you to talk to me. I'll ring for some tea.'

For a few minutes they discussed Megan Smythe's wedding and then Annis told him about the rehearsal that she'd just attended.

'They're a wonderful group of youngsters. I'm fond of young Millie,' he commented. 'The problem is, her mother's very possessive and proud. She's had a hard life and she's very ambitious for Millie — but the girl must be allowed to be ambitious for herself. She's got her father's sunny nature — pity he died so young.'

'Did you know him well, Bryn?' she asked, intrigued.

'Well, I met him on several occasions.'

Tea arrived at that point, and Annis poured him a cup and then passed the cakes. He asked her a few rather searching questions about her job in London.

'There's something you're not telling me, Annis,' he said, surveying her with his astute blue eyes. 'You know, I have the distinct feeling that you don't like that job of yours in London very much, do you?'

She hesitated for a moment. 'You could always read me like a book, Bryn. It was OK until recently, but then there was a change of management and I don't get on with my new boss.'

Bryn's eyes twinkled. 'So, do you think you could consider working here on a more permanent basis?'

Annis thought about this and then nodded. 'I thought it would be impossible, but now that I've been here for a while, I've slipped back into the routine and it's not nearly as difficult as I thought it would be.'

'Annis, I'd welcome you back with open arms, you know that.'

There was a knock on the door and Ross looked into the room.

'Oh! I thought I'd ask you to sign a few cheques so I can get them in the post first thing tomorrow, but I see you're busy, so I'll come back later.'

'You will not!' Bryn Freeman's eyebrows bristled. 'Annis, could you make us some more tea, please? You'll find everything you want in the kitchenette. I'm sure Ross could do with a cup.'

'Make it a mug — I'm parched,' said Ross, smiling at her.

Annis stayed in the kitchen longer than she needed to in order to give them time to deal with things, then she brought through the tea tray and set it in front of Ross.

'I'll leave you to it,' she said, making for the door.

'Are you two deliberately trying to avoid each other?' Bryn demanded. 'Sit down, Annis — there's nothing that Ross and I have to discuss that you can't hear. Anyway, we've just about finished. Ross, Annis thinks I ought to make myself useful downstairs — she says it's time I got off my backside and did something worthwhile!'

'I did not!' Annis's cheeks flamed. 'You told me you were bored and so I merely suggested you might like to become a little more involved.'

'Actually I think Annis might have a point,' said Ross, smiling. 'A few hours a week downstairs might make all the difference . . . '

'To whom?' Bryn Freeman asked. 'Tell you what, I'll give it a bit of thought, but I'm not so steady on my pins these days, so I can't go gallivanting about too much.'

Annis and Ross eventually took their leave together and, half-way down the stairs, he paused and stood looking at her.

'I'm a bit tied up at the moment, Annis — we've got some delegates arriving shortly for tomorrow's conference,' he said. 'But it seems to me that we never have time to talk other than in snatches, so how about coming for a drink in the bar tonight?'

'So that you can take me to task over what I've suggested to Bryn? No, thank you!' she said spiritedly.

'You don't have a very high opinion

of me, do you?' Ross looked genuinely hurt by her outburst. 'Actually, you couldn't be more wrong. I happen to think it's an excellent idea. In the short time you've been here, Bryn's perked up and come out of his shell. It was kind of you to take the time and trouble to come up to tell him about the play rehearsal. I know he appreciated it.' He paused.

'Look, I owe you an apology for last night. It's none of my business who you go out with.'

'You're right there. You're behaving like a bossy older brother,' she told him.

He was standing so close to her that if she attempted to move, she would have to brush past him. He reached out and removed a piece of grass from her sweatshirt sleeve and she caught her breath, realising with a shock that there was some kind of magnetism between them.

'Yes, well, we look out for one another around here, like one big family. I thought you would have known that.' He looked straight into her eyes for a moment. 'I must go. There are a couple of things I've got to attend to right now, but if you want, I'll see you in the bar at eight — I can't make it any earlier, I'm afraid.'

She stood staring after him as he took the remainder of the stairs two at a time and hurried off down the corridor. His cologne lingered in the air, fresh and clean. She realised then that there was no way she would ever think of him as a brother . . .

⋆ ⋆ ⋆

After supper, she went for a brisk walk around the grounds, making a mental note to ask Ross about a key for the garden. And she decided that she *would* go to the bar, just for half an hour or so.

Ross was there already and, while he was getting their drinks, she watched him chatting to some people who'd arrived early for the conference. He'd changed into a crisp white shirt and light trousers and looked every bit the confident businessman. He had all the social graces too, and she wondered if he felt that it was his duty to entertain her, or if it was just that he was at a loose end that evening.

'I'm glad you could make it, Annis,' he said, sitting down opposite her. 'I wanted to welcome you personally to the team. I feel it's long overdue — and to give you this, rather belatedly.'

'What is it?' She looked curiously at the pack he had pushed into her hands.

'Inside you'll find a staff card for the swimming pool, some discount vouchers, and keys to the gardens.'

She laughed, and he raised his eyebrows in surprise.

'What have I said?'

'Oh, it's just that I managed to get locked in the other day, after you'd left me!' She didn't explain how she'd got out.

They talked about general things after that, about London and about some of the exhibitions, films and plays she'd seen in recent months, including a production at The Globe Theatre which he had seen too.

Presently, they were joined by some of the other staff, and Annis was surprised to discover that a couple of hours had gone past without her noticing. She went off to bed in a much happier frame of mind.

* * *

The next day and a half were hectic. Sally insisted on getting up to date with as much as possible before she left for her course. She worked at a frenetic pace and by the time Annis finally persuaded her to go home at around half past one on Tuesday afternoon, they were both feeling tired.

Annis decided to have a short break and a much deserved cup of coffee. She had just poured it when Ross stormed into the office.

'Where's Sally?'

'She's gone home. Is there anything I

can do to help?'

'Jeff Hughes has just been in to see me saying that one of the clients has made a complaint about the cost of the wedding stationery. He says he was promised a special discount which he hasn't been given. Look, here's the invoice — the client has obviously been charged the rate for a more expensive package. The number of times this sort of mistake has happened recently — it must be inefficiency on someone's part. And the florist has rung to tell me that they haven't received payment for the last few wedding orders.'

Annis's heart sank.

'OK, I'll look into it just as soon as I've had my coffee. Would you like a cup?'

'No, thank you. I don't have time for a break. Let me know as soon as you come up with an explanation, Miss Fuller.'

His dark eyes met hers and for a moment held them in a steely grip.

Annis calmly finished her coffee,

watching as Ross went over to a filing cabinet and began searching through one of the drawers.

'Please just leave it with me, Mr Hadley,' she said as he straightened up. 'I'll get back to you just as soon as I've tracked down the missing invoices.'

'See that you do.' Ross had a file in his hand. 'They're not in the usual place, I've just looked, but in any case, I need this file for something else.' And he hurried out of the room.

Annis took her time. She was fuming over Ross's attitude and decided that he would just have to wait his turn. She had another job listed for the afternoon which took priority.

She finished off what she was doing and eventually located the missing invoices stuffed at the back of one of the filing cabinet drawers. She was puzzled, knowing that Sally was far too efficient to have merely overlooked them.

Attaching a memo to the invoices, Annis took them next door, to Ross's office. Finding that he wasn't around, she handed them to the young girl who job-shared with Stella.

Annis was relieved when the afternoon finally came to an end. Locking up carefully, she went back to her room to have a shower before dinner.

She was a little later than usual going into the dining-room, and found it crowded. Collecting her meal, she stood looking around for a vacant seat and, seeing her predicament, Ross came to her rescue.

'You're more than welcome to join me again, if you can bear to. There are things I need to say to you anyway.'

Reluctantly she went across to his table and for a few moments they ate in silence, until at last he spoke.

'Look, I owe you an apology. Thanks for those invoices — Amy gave them to me. I'm afraid things have been a bit fraught recently, but you're a guest of Bryn's and there's no excuse for me to vent my feelings on you.'

'Right, that's cleared the air then,'

she said briskly. 'Apology accepted. I don't know how those invoices came to be overlooked, and I agree that it shouldn't have happened, but they've come to light now.'

'Yes, but it shouldn't have been down to you to sort it out. Anyway, thanks, and remember, you can always come to one of us if there are any more problems during Sally's absence.'

'You sound as if you're expecting that there will be.' Annis cut into her onion and pepper tart. 'That's the sort of attitude that makes people feel as if they're not trusted. Fortunately, Tristan doesn't seem to share your concern.'

'Really? I wouldn't be too sure about that if I were you. The difference between Tristan and myself is that I speak my mind and he uses the kid glove approach . . . Dessert?'

'I'll get my own, thanks.'

She was annoyed with him, but she knew that she was handling the situation badly. She needed to get Ross on her side.

When he returned with a loaded tray, she went up to the hatch herself and selected a yoghurt, fruit and tea.

He raised an eyebrow. 'Slimming?'

'No, but I've been over-indulging lately. The food here is rather too good!'

'I should hope so. We've a reputation to maintain — besides, feed the staff well and they'll work well.'

'Over-indulge them and they'll fall asleep on the job!' she quipped.

He laughed and she realised again what an attractive man he was when he relaxed.

'I usually go for a walk after dinner when I can manage it,' he said as they finished their meal, 'and I've noticed you doing the same — d'you fancy joining me?'

She was surprised, but realised this might be the very opportunity she needed to get to know him better.

'Around the grounds, do you mean?' she asked.

'No, I was actually thinking of cutting through the orchard to the church and then returning via the village.'

'Lovely — if you can wait while I pop up to say goodnight to Bryn.'

* * *

Half an hour later they set off. Annis had quickly changed into jeans and a sweatshirt and Ross had pulled on a light sweater.

'You didn't spend long with Bryn,' he commented.

'No, Arthur Smythe had turned up to play chess. He's still talking about the wedding in glowing terms.'

'Good — that's what we need to hear.'

They walked along the boundary of the Mill for a few moments in companionable silence.

'What else do you do in your free time, apart from going for walks?' she asked.

'Oh, I try to fit in a swim most mornings, and now and again I have a game of snooker, or a drink in the bar. I spend some time with Bryn, too.'

'And what do you get up to on your days off?'

'If ever I do manage to get a day off then I try to get away — down to the coast, perhaps, or off to visit friends. As you probably know, my family live in the north of England, so I need more than a day or two to go up there.'

They had reached the stile leading into the orchard and, hopping across in one agile movement, he took Annis's hand to help her over. Again, she felt her fingers tingle at the contact.

She resolved to get a firm grip on herself and keep in her mind that although he hadn't said as much, it was evident that Ross was more than a little involved with Stella, and unfortunately for Annis, she had been down that path before.

The orchard was a haven of peace and Annis took a deep breath of fresh air. It was a glorious evening and still pleasantly warm.

Suddenly Ross pointed. 'Look, Annis! There goes a fox!'

They stood watching the creature until it shimmied under the fence and disappeared into the meadow beyond.

'The apples will be ripe shortly,' commented Ross. 'They're absolutely delicious.'

Annis gave him a reproving look. 'But the orchard doesn't belong to the Mill.'

'I know that, Miss Goody Two-Shoes! But the daughter of the farmer that it *does* belong to, got married at the Mill a couple of years ago, and her father's sent us a couple of boxes of apples every year since.'

'Always got your eye on the main chance, haven't you?' she said, tongue in cheek, wondering if she appeared as self-righteous to everyone else as she apparently did to him.

'Of course.' He grinned and took her arm. 'That's good business acumen.'

They walked into the field beyond the orchard where the corn was ready for harvesting.

'I love this time of year — poppies and cow parsley,' she said.

'Me too. But don't you find it too hot at this time of year in London?'

'Yes, but I work in an air-conditioned office, and there are the parks and gardens.'

'But no cornfields or cow parsley! Do you enjoy your work?'

She considered.

'It's interesting — busy and varied.'

'Are you in the same line of business there as this?' he asked casually.

'No — I work in a planning department.'

'That must be interesting. And do you have your own house?'

'In London? You must be joking! I share a flat with a couple of friends. It's a bit small, but it's adequate.'

When they reached the edge of the field, Ross leaned against the gate and turned to face her.

'Well, Annis, tell me: if you had the opportunity to change things — what innovative ideas would you introduce at

Heathercote Mill?'

So that's why he had asked her to go for a walk with him. So that he could carry on sounding her out.

'I've told you — I think it's in danger of becoming impersonal. It's people that you're dealing with in this business, not things.'

'Yes, you've made your point, and now I'm asking you what you would do about it.'

'Well, the way things are at present, the staff don't seem to be working together as a team, and that doesn't make for good morale. Everything seems so fragmented.'

Ross was listening intently.

'Yes, I see, but it's important to strike a happy balance. You've already said that you feel there's too much interference, but we can't have it both ways. Remember, Tristan and I are responsible to Bryn for every decision we make and we need to be able to assure him that everything is ticking over in a satisfactory manner.'

'And is it?' Annis removed her sandal and shook out a small stone. 'For one thing, Sally seems in danger of losing her confidence. I really can't believe it's her fault so many things have gone wrong lately, and yet you and Tristan always seem to be on her back.'

Ross's eyes glinted and she wondered if she'd gone too far.

'Yes, well, we'll see if she's feeling more relaxed when she comes back from the course,' he said.

They had reached the churchyard and stopped to admire the view from there, across the weald of Kent. The churchyard was a tranquil spot — and it was also the place where Andrew was buried. Ross sensed her sudden tension and realised what was wrong.

'Annis, I'm so sorry — it was thoughtless of me to bring you here.'

She was trembling in spite of the warm evening. 'It's OK. I just suddenly realised where we are . . . and I've never seen Andrew's grave.'

‘Would you like to?’ Ross put his arm gently round her shoulders.

She nodded. ‘I’ve put it off for too long.’

He took her hand and led her down a slope to the grave, and she stood in silence for a moment, reading the inscription. There were some fresh carnations in a vase.

‘Are the flowers — does Stella visit?’

‘I’m sure she does, but those are from Bryn. I brought them here myself on Sunday. Would you like some time on your own?’

She shook her head. ‘No — no, thanks, but I’m glad I came. He liked this place. Can we go now?’

For a few moments they walked in silence down the lane that led to the village.

‘Andrew lived life to the full, Annis,’ Ross said at last. ‘What happened was a terrible tragedy, but he would want you to move on.’

‘I’ve tried that,’ she said bitterly. ‘I thought I could handle it, and most days I can, but just now and then it all comes flooding back . . . ' There was a lump in her throat and she turned away.

He didn't say anything further, but she was glad of his company.

'Do you like it here, Ross?' she asked as they approached Heronsbridge.

'Yes, I like Heathercote Mill, and Heronsbridge, and it's amazing how quickly one adapts.'

'Yes, it's a friendly community for the most part.'

When they arrived back at the Mill he said, 'Thanks for your company. I don't know about you, but I could do with a long cool drink. Care to join me?'

She was tired, but she was also reluctant to spend the rest of the evening on her own.

'Thanks — just for a short while,' she told him.

Tristan was already in the bar, sitting in a corner in deep conversation with Vicki.

When Ross returned with their drinks, Annis said curiously, 'Does Vicki live in?'

'Vicki?' He cast his eyes in their direction, his face expressionless. 'No, but she spends a night or two here sometimes if she has to make an early start, which is why you've seen her at breakfast once or twice. Vicki's worth her weight in gold — unlike her sister, Kelly, who left Sally in the lurch a few weeks back.'

'What became of Kelly?' asked Annis casually.

'D'you know, I'm not too sure — I'll have to ask Vicki. Kelly certainly didn't like working here.'

Just then one of the conference delegates came across with a query for Ross, and then one or two others joined their table. There was soon an animated discussion going on about the state of the economy, and after a few minutes, too tired to take any part in it, Annis made her excuses and went back to her room.

* * *

The following morning, Sally went off on her course and Annis hoped that things would go smoothly during her absence.

The next couple of days fell into a repeat pattern of the previous week, and Annis began to feel as if she had never been away from Heathercote Mill.

On Thursday morning, she decided to phone her boss in London. He was surprisingly reasonable and she put the receiver down knowing that she had burnt her bridges.

She had not even told Sally that she'd actually taken three weeks' leave, not two, knowing that if things didn't work out here she could at least spend some time with her parents before returning to London.

That morning, however, she had made a decision and had given in her notice.

Her boss didn't seem surprised, but

he told her that she would be required to work out her full month's notice as there were too many people going off on holiday during August for her to be allowed to leave any earlier. He had, however, come up with a solution, telling her that Fiona, who was at present standing in for Annis, could probably be persuaded to carry on, with a view to taking over Annis's job permanently in a month's time. If Annis would be prepared to work out her notice by covering for those on holiday, then she could do flexi-time, leaving at two o'clock on Friday afternoons.

It was an acceptable compromise. It meant that while she was working out her notice, she would be able to come back to Heronsbridge each weekend and lend a hand, easing herself out of the London job and into this one.

Now all that remained was for her to have another word with Bryn.

Is Stella Spying?

Annis had just returned from a hasty lunch, and was filing some letters and receipts, when there was a brief knock at the door and Stella Freeman walked in. Annis was unprepared for her visitor but quickly composed herself. The older woman looked chic and self-possessed.

'Hello, Annis. Ross told me you're holding the fort while Sally's away on her course. He suggested I pop over to see how you're getting on. We haven't had much time for a chat, have we?'

Annis continued with what she was doing, surprised that Ross had sent Stella over, but determined not to show it.

'Is there anything in particular you want to know?'

Stella smiled. 'I've been wondering whatever possessed you to return here after all this time — curiosity or nostalgia?'

'Neither of those things,' Annis told her honestly. 'I had a bit of leave to use up, Sally needed a hand, and I hadn't seen Bryn for a long time, so it was an ideal opportunity to visit. Now, if you don't mind, I'm rather busy . . . '

'Oh, don't mind me, just carry on with what you're doing.'

Stella wandered over to the coffee maker and poured herself a cup and then perched elegantly on one of the chairs, legs crossed.

'I thought I'd just drop in to see how you're coping.'

'Fine, thanks. I gather you work here part-time nowadays, as Ross's personal assistant?'

'Yes — Ross has been such a tower of strength to me during the past years. He kept in touch with me all the time I was in Canada and after, when I returned to London. I'd never have come back here if it hadn't been for him, and now that I have, things are working out really well for me.'

'I'm pleased to hear it, and I'm glad that you're keeping well. Now, if you'll excuse me . . . '

So, Ross had been responsible for Stella returning to Heronsbridge, had he? Annis realised that, for some reason, the idea of the two of them being such good friends troubled her.

'How would you say this side of the business is doing?' Stella asked now, setting down her cup and saucer.

So that was it! Annis felt the anger rising in her and was aware that Stella was watching her keenly. Well, she would not give the other woman the satisfaction of seeing that she was riled.

'Thriving. It's better than ever — in spite of all the media's claims that weddings aren't so popular these days. Of course, Bryn has the details of the financial side, but you know that already.'

'Of course. I'm sure you're aware that I'm a shareholder in the company.'

The older woman's eyes narrowed. 'But I've had the distinct impression recently that Sally hasn't had her finger on the pulse. Things haven't been quite up to the standard that one expects.'

Annis was incensed, but she was determined to keep her cool.

'Really? I can't imagine what gave you that idea. And you came to sound me out while Sally isn't here to defend herself, did you, Stella? Well, everything is just fine — running like clockwork. You can rest assured on that score.'

A slight colour tinged Stella's cheeks.

'I admit I was hoping that with Sally away we might be able to get to the bottom of what's been going wrong.'

Silently seething, Annis poured herself a cup of coffee, and found the biscuits that Sally kept in the top drawer. Then, with great self control, she sat down in front of Stella and brought her up to date with the weddings that were scheduled for that week.

'So you see, Mrs Freeman, there's nothing to be concerned about. Everything is running smoothly, and once Sally has had a few days' break, she'll return refreshed.'

Annis had spoken these words carefully, watching Stella's face.

'So you think that things might have been getting on top of Sally? I know she's your friend, but you can speak freely to me.'

Stella selected a biscuit for herself and nibbled at it daintily.

'Thank you, I'll remember that.' Annis was puzzled as to what exactly Stella was doing there, but had a flash of sudden inspiration. 'I have a potential client coming at three-thirty but, before then, I want to check on a couple of things with Madame Cecile. There's a new enterprise that Sally and I have been thinking about. Perhaps you'd like to come with me?'

She had caught Stella's attention.

'What new enterprise? Bryn hasn't said anything to me.'

'Oh, that's because it's only an embryo of an idea at present, but I'm sure it would be all right if I ran it by you.'

* * *

Stella accompanied her to the boutique and stood by impatiently while Annis discussed a couple of orders with Madame Cecile. Then Annis took Stella into the nearby empty unit.

'I understand there have been a number of suggestions for this empty unit, but nothing has got off the ground. Sally and I have put forward the possibility of having a milliner's shop in here.'

Stella frowned. 'Don't you think enough space has already been given over to the wedding business? Surely there could be better use made of it?'

'Well, it's only an idea, but it does seem a pity not to utilise the space.'

Annis held her breath. Would Stella reveal any hint that there was any management opposition to the expansion of the wedding business?

Stella was unimpressed by Annis and Sally's plans. 'I'm aware that this is a wonderful venue for weddings — I was married here myself, after all, but nowadays it's possible to get married in a variety of beautiful locations and there could be other, equally good, uses for the grounds if a bit less space was given over to the wedding enterprise.'

Annis realised that she was on the right lines.

'Yes, I've often thought myself what potential there is here. You've obviously got a few ideas. Would you like to share them with me?'

Stella gave a tinkling little laugh. 'So that you can repeat it all back to Sally and John Barnes? I don't think so!'

She stepped outside of the unit and Annis followed her.

'There's been far too much money spent on developing the wedding business in recent years,' Stella continued, 'and now it's the turn of . . . '

She broke off as Tristan came along the path towards them.

'So there you are! I've been looking for both of you! Ross is champing at the bit wondering where you are, Stella. You've obviously done what you're always having a go at me about — turned off your mobile. Annis, there are a couple of potential customers in reception who've turned up early for their appointment.'

Annis set off for reception. From the way Stella had looked daggers at Tristan, she wondered if Ross really had sent Stella to check up on her.

Annis went into reception to find a young couple drinking coffee and not at all concerned that they'd had to wait for a few moments. Presently, having chosen the package that suited them best, they said they would return with the bride-to-be's father to pay the necessary deposit.

When they had gone, Annis entered the details of their package on the computer, removed the disk and carefully checked the appointments book for the following day. She was preparing to leave the office when Tristan came in.

'Oh, good, I've just caught you . . . Busy afternoon?'

'Yes, it has been quite hectic,' she agreed as she locked the desk drawer.

'It probably wasn't helped by my sister breathing down your neck.'

It was as if he could read her mind.

'Stella doesn't seem to like the wedding enterprise much, does she?' she couldn't help saying.

'That's hardly surprising, is it?' He leaned against her desk. 'Think about it — she was married here such a short time ago and lost Andrew in such tragic circumstances. The trauma is still here.'

For a moment, Annis felt that she'd been insensitive. Perhaps she had misjudged Stella.

'Well, I realise that, Tristan. It must be very difficult for her. Actually, I was surprised to learn that she had come back here to work.'

'That's what she's just said about

you,' he said quietly. 'Anyway, enough of that . . . How about coming out to dinner with me this evening? Somewhere we can relax, eat good food, and dance?'

'Is Vicki on duty then?' she asked him naughtily.

He looked startled and then gave a little laugh. 'Oh, Vicki and I are just good friends — nothing more. So, will you come?'

She found herself agreeing, against her better judgement, and hurried off to shower and change into a sapphire blue sundress which she hoped would be appropriate. Snatching up a lightweight jacket, she made her way to reception.

Crossing the hall, she encountered Ross, who raised his eyebrows.

'Very fetching — going somewhere special?' he asked.

'Out with me,' Tristan told him smoothly, suddenly appearing at her side.

She wondered if it was her imagination or if a swift look of annoyance crossed Ross's face. 'I see — well, enjoy yourselves.'

'We will,' Tristan told him and caught Annis's arm. For some reason, she felt uncomfortable, as if she oughtn't to have accepted the invitation. But she couldn't see what business it was of Ross's.

* * *

The place Tristan had chosen was trendy, and rather too noisy for her liking, but the food was good. She again realised that he was good company and he soon had her chuckling at anecdotes about his work as a waiter during his student days. It was apparent that he enjoyed an audience and for some time seemed content with a rather one-sided conversation.

In between courses he asked her to dance and, as they whirled round the floor, he fired a few questions at her about her job in London and her plans for the future.

'Oh, I never plan too far ahead,' she told him honestly. 'I tend to live from day to day.'

'Rumour has it that you're thinking of coming back to Heronsbridge permanently.'

'You shouldn't listen to rumours,' she told him lightly, wondering who had been gossiping.

The dance ended and he led her back to the table.

'Annis, there are a few things I ought to tell you about myself before you hear them from someone else,' he said abruptly. 'You may wonder why Ross and I don't exactly hit it off.'

She shrugged. 'You're both very different personalities, but, as you've said, you muddle along.'

He nodded. 'Yes, but there's a bit more to it than that, I'm afraid. You see, I've got a bit of a past. I was pretty wild when I was in my teens. My grandfather financed my schooling and paid to put me through university and I repaid him by getting into debt and dropping out before I took my finals. I went off back-packing instead.'

Tristan shrugged ruefully. 'Ross knew me when I was younger, so it's small wonder he doesn't have a very high opinion of me. I never did repay my grandfather his hard-earned cash.

'My father fell out with him, as you probably know. Dad didn't want to join the business, and he encouraged me to get all I could out of the old man because he thought he wouldn't inherit a penny piece himself. And I'm ashamed to say that I did just that.'

He did indeed look somewhat ashamed of himself.

'That's why, although Stella was given shares in the business on her wedding day and later inherited Andrew's, I just have the trust fund. Not that I'm not grateful!' he insisted, then paused.

'It's also why I didn't come to see my grandfather before he died,' he said regretfully, 'and that's something else I'll have to live with.'

'Yes, I see,' Annis said. 'But you're here now, supporting Stella, and from what I can tell, you and Ross are making a good job of running the conference centre between you.'

Tristan sighed.

'The thing is, Annis, I'm a different person nowadays. I've matured, but somehow I don't know how to prove it. You see, Bryn Freeman is a nice enough old chap, but he's a bit like an ostrich: his head's buried in the sand where change is concerned. And Ross is steady and dependable, and not prepared to take a gamble.'

Annis thought she could see where the conversation was leading.

'OK, so what is it you're trying to say?'

'Oh, I've got so many ideas, but I need to get a few people on my side.' He smiled winningly. 'Now you seem like a lady with a fresh approach and I gather you've got Bryn Freeman's ear. He'd listen to you.'

Annis shook her head. 'I don't want

to get involved in your schemes, Tristan. Look, why don't you go and see him yourself with your ideas? I'm sure he'd listen.'

'I'm not just talking about utilising an empty unit here, Annis,' Tristan retorted. 'The problem is, Bryn's the majority share-holder and that means he always gets the final say when it comes to change.'

Annis looked at her watch. 'It's time I was getting back, Tristan — I've a busy day ahead of me tomorrow. Dinner was great and I've had a lovely time. I'm sorry I can't help you with your new ideas, but unless I know exactly what you're proposing I can't really advise . . . '

'And unless I can be sure of your support, I can't tell you.'

He drove her back to the Mill rather too fast for her liking and practically in silence, but as they reached the cobbled forecourt to the Mill she felt him relax.

Pulling up, he leaned across. 'I've enjoyed this evening, Annis. Think about what I've said. I reckon we'd make a good team!' And he kissed her firmly on the mouth.

Ross was in the reception area as Annis entered the Mill. He raised his eyebrows. 'Back so soon? I thought you'd be dancing the night away.'

The urge to confide in him was strong, but how could she be sure that he and Tristan weren't hatching some scheme together and trying to get everyone to agree to it behind Sally's back? If only she could get some idea of what that scheme might be.

'I've a busy day tomorrow and need my beauty sleep,' she told him.

'Then I'll wish you sweet dreams,' he said.

But sleep evaded her, and she lay awake wondering just what Tristan had in mind. When she finally fell into a fitful sleep, it was to dream that all the grounds had been taken over by a housing estate, supermarket, and a new school!

* * *

Annis had started going for a swim before work each morning. Sometimes she was joined by one or two of the staff, all of whom seemed friendly.

On Friday morning when she came out from the changing room, she saw someone on the diving board and realised it was Ross.

She stood watching him for a few moments, noting the tanned body and rippling muscles. As he dived in, she realised that Ross really wasn't like Andrew at all. Andrew had disliked swimming and she had had to coax him into the water. Andrew had not been so powerfully built as Ross either, and certainly not so athletic.

'Come and join me — the water's wonderful,' Ross called to her.

She jumped into the pool and swam across to him, and for a few moments they swam side by side.

'You're pretty good, Annis — fancy a race?'

She nodded and made for the end of the pool. He was by far the stronger swimmer, but she suspected he was holding back so that they could finish almost together.

'That was good,' he told her. 'I like the swimsuit, by the way — shows off those lovely long legs of yours.' He said it matter-of-factly, but she found herself colouring at the unexpected compliment.

'I'd better get changed — I don't want to be late for breakfast,' she murmured.

Ross climbed out of the pool and held out a hand to help her. Then, fetching a couple of towels and passing one to her, he marched off towards the changing cubicles without uttering another word.

That day was set to be amazingly busy.

There was a wedding ceremony that afternoon, but the reception was being held elsewhere. Despite this, it still took a surprising amount of work to make sure that everything ran smoothly, so Annis was excused from the short lunch-time meeting with Bryn Freeman.

The wedding ceremony was a simple but delightful affair. The bride was an older lady who looked quite lovely in a cream silk suit with a bouquet of cream and pink roses. Her one bridesmaid wore a dress of pale pink print. Everything went according to plan, and afterwards Annis sighed with relief.

There were two ceremonies booked for the following day, and each was to have a finger buffet reception lasting two to three hours, but no evening function.

By the time Annis had made sure everything was on target, from marquees and champagne to flowers and cakes, it was mid-evening.

After a hasty supper, she went up to see Bryn, intending to sound him out about her staying on at the Mill. As usual he was pleased to see her and she spent fifteen minutes filling him in on the activities of the day and the schedule for Saturday.

'Well, you seem to have got on top of everything, lass. Well done!'

She took a deep breath and explained the real purpose of her visit.

Bryn listened intently, nodding his wise old head. When she had finished, he fixed her with his bright blue eyes.

'You've certainly given it some thought, Annis, and if you're sure it's what you want . . . Of course, you do realise it can only be a temporary position to begin with. We're going to have to wait to see what Zoe wants to do when her maternity leave is up.'

'Yes, but it would give me time to think, away from London.'

'Between you and me,' said Bryn, 'I've a feeling that once the baby is born, Zoe won't want to come back here full-time, so she might be prepared to do a job share. Anyway, we shall see. It's going to be a mighty busy time for you for the next month or so, Annis.

Are you certain that you can handle the pace?'

'I thrive on hard work,' she assured him, her eyes shining with enthusiasm. 'Anyway, I'll have my Sundays more or less free, and naturally I won't expect to be on the payroll until I'm working here on a permanent basis.'

'Oh, I think we can come to some arrangement. If you can bring a smile back to Sally's face then you'll be worth your weight in gold. She's been so down these past weeks. Now, how about having a cup of coffee with me and watching that wildlife programme on TV?'

* * *

It was after ten-thirty when Annis finally left Bryn. She came down the stairs in a rush and nearly collided with Ross at the bottom. He straightened her up.

'Just the person I needed to see! Can you spare me a few moments? Come on, let's go for a walk.'

'But it's nearly eleven o'clock!' Annis looked at him as if he were mad.

'Just a stroll around the grounds? We've got a bit of a crisis on our hands and I'm wondering if you've got any bright ideas.'

As Annis wondered what had happened now, Ross took her by the arm and led her outside. It was a beautiful moonlit night.

'Chef's been called away — his father-in-law up in Scotland has died suddenly.'

'Oh, poor Luis. Well, I'm sure the sous chef will manage admirably. He's been trained well.'

'I'm sure he has, but unfortunately he's gone to Paris with his fiancée for a much deserved break.'

'Well, not to worry — you've still got Niall and he's pretty reliable.'

Annis heard Ross sigh and her heart sank.

'What's happened to him?' she asked.

'He took umbrage at something

Stella said to him, and he and his wife walked out this evening. I'll try to talk them round after they've had a chance to cool off.'

'What did Stella say?' Annis asked.

'Apparently she told him that the pastry on this evening's pie tasted like cardboard!' Ross's mouth twitched and then he started laughing. 'I'm sorry, but actually she was right, and she was the only person to dare say so. He was definitely having an off day!'

Annis joined in with his laughter, but then he sobered.

'They do say laughter is the best medicine,' he said, 'but really, it's quite a serious situation. I've e-mailed all the agencies we use, so let's hope they come up with someone suitable, but in the meantime we've got a bit of a problem.'

'Oh, it'll be all right — Sally's due back in a few days' time.'

'So?' he asked in a puzzled tone.

'So, both of us have done cordon bleu cookery courses, and while we wouldn't pretend to have the expertise of the regular chefs, we could get by for a short time.'

'Annis, you're like a breath of fresh air! What about the weddings?'

'We've two ceremonies tomorrow, but they're fairly low-key affairs — around fifty guests each with a few hours' grace between them. The small marquees are up already, as you can see. The menus are fairly straightforward, and I've no doubt that the remainder of the catering staff can cope admirably.'

She heard his sigh of relief.

'We've a big conference coming in at the beginning of next week, and some of the delegates will be arriving on Sunday afternoon,' he murmured. 'Oh, well, I guess we can get by somehow.'

'Of course we can . . . it'll all work out OK, you'll see.'

'You know something, Annis? I'm beginning to wonder how we ever managed without you.'

'You didn't think that when I first

came here — you couldn't wait to see the back of me,' she pointed out.

'Yes, well, I'm the first to admit if I make a mistake. I know I took a bit of convincing and I'm sorry I was so hostile towards you.'

They were walking by the lake and the solar lights were reflected in the water. His arm rested lightly round her waist and suddenly he caught her to him and dropped a gentle kiss on her lips.

Her heart pounded. She realised it was only meant as an apology, and was taken aback at the intensity of her feelings.

'Don't worry, I won't make a habit of that,' he told her, 'but at least it's too dark for you to look at me and see Andrew.'

Annis's mind was in turmoil. She realised that if she wasn't careful, she could fall for this man in a big way — and not just because he reminded her of Andrew. She had stopped thinking that soon after her arrival at Heronsbridge.

They walked back to the Mill in silence, and she wished she could at least hint that she had begun to accept Ross for himself, although she would never forget Andrew. He had been a part of her life that had, for the most part, been happy.

* * *

The next morning was glorious. Annis had a quick dip in the pool and then went to the kitchen to see if they needed any help. Ross was there already. He looked up and gave her a devastating smile that sent a frisson dancing down her spine.

'I've explained to everyone that until we can get some more help, they must just continue the best they can. In the meantime, Lisa here is in charge and I've told her you'll lend a hand, Annis, as and when you can.'

It didn't take too long for Annis to check the food for the two wedding receptions, the first of which was to be at one o'clock.

Staff breakfasts were in hand and everything — on the surface, at least — seemed to have an air of calm.

The morning flew past. There was no apparent hitch with the first of the two ceremonies.

When the first reception was underway, Annis slipped back into the kitchen and, donning an overall and cap, helped with decorating desserts and arranging quantities of miniature savoury tartlets and chicken pieces on platters for the next reception.

Lisa was expertly piping cream into tiny pastries and éclairs. They had been working against the clock all morning, but now things were coming together at last.

Suddenly the kitchen doors swung open and Stella strode in.

'Come along, everyone, the guests will be heading towards the marquee at any moment. Everything ought to be ready by now.'

She suddenly noticed Annis and her eyes widened. ‘What on earth are you doing here? Shouldn’t you be outside?’

Annis explained briefly that the first reception was already underway and the second one wasn’t due to begin for a couple of hours yet, and then turned her attention back to what she was doing.

Stella’s eyes narrowed. ‘That’s as may be but this is most irregular — I shall speak to Mr Hadley. Meanwhile, I suggest you return to the marquee area immediately.’

‘Certainly, Mrs Freeman — but in that case, perhaps you’d care to take over here? It’s all hands on deck today. I volunteered to step in since I’ve got a cordon bleu qualification, but if I’m needed elsewhere . . . ’

The whole of the kitchen staff watched and waited with interest.

A flush of colour swept across Stella’s cheeks. Her green eyes glittered with anger as they met Annis’s, but she spoke coolly.

'I'm afraid I can't be spared, so I suppose you'll have to stay for the time being. But I shall look into the situation.'

Turning abruptly, a furious look on her face, Stella swept out of the room.

'Why didn't you tell her Mr Hadley had sanctioned you being here?' asked Lisa, looking worried.

'I wasn't aware that the kitchen came under her jurisdiction,' Annis replied calmly, and was surprised to encounter one or two shocked stares.

'But Mrs Freeman is management and she's Mr Hadley's PA,' Lisa said in hushed tones, staring at Annis with a mixture of fear and shocked admiration on her face.

'Yes, I know that, but it doesn't give her the right to throw her weight around in your kitchen, does it?' said Annis. 'Now then, shall I take some of this stuff over to the marquee?'

'It's about time someone stood up to that Mrs Freeman,' one of the waiters said as they entered the marquee. 'She's got too much influence; for some reason, people are in awe of her.'

'Well, I'm not,' Annis said, 'and I'm sure Chef isn't either.'

* * *

Both receptions went smoothly, and Lisa's cooking was praised by several of the guests. Afterwards, Annis helped to clear away, and then assisted Lisa with the staff meal. Much later still, the kitchen staff sat down thankfully to their own supper in the kitchen.

'It's been great having you here today,' Lisa told Annis. 'It's good to find someone who's prepared to muck in at a moment's notice, isn't it, guys?'

The rest of the kitchen staff nodded. Annis knew four of them from years back when Lisa had been only a junior. Although they were friendly enough now, she had felt, back then, that there was some kind of barrier between them.

'Things have certainly altered since

the last time I was here,' Annis ventured to say now.

'And not all of the changes have been for the better,' said Harry, one of the porters. 'It's not nearly so easy-going here as it used to be. There seem to be too many chiefs these days.'

'Everything's OK providing we tow the line and stick to the rules,' Millie added.

'Well, you've got to have a system, otherwise where would you be? But we don't have so much of a laugh nowadays,' someone else said.

'We could have done with you being around a few years back, Annis — times were rough then,' Lisa added.

There was a note of reproach in her voice and Annis couldn't blame her. Suddenly she realised just how selfish she'd been, so wrapped up in her own misery. She hadn't spared a thought for the others, or bothered to enquire how they'd coped during those months directly after the fire when the Mill had been closed and they'd been out of work.

She knew that Harry had a disabled mother and that one of the ladies cared for her young granddaughter. Each had their own problems, and she suddenly realised that they must all be wondering why she hadn't bothered to come back after the fire to see how they were all coping.

Ross came into the kitchen just then, full of praise for the way the day had gone.

'You can be proud of yourselves. There have been a number of compliments. Tomorrow should be very much easier. About twenty guests are arriving late afternoon for the conference on Monday. The rest of them won't be coming until Monday morning. We'll run through the menus tomorrow, Lisa, and thanks, Annis, for your input today.' He nodded to Annis, smiling. 'It's good to know we can rely on you in a crisis.'

Annis met Harry's eyes, and suddenly she couldn't bear the unspoken accusation any longer. She got to her feet and with a murmured excuse went from the room.

A few minutes later, she found herself walking round the lake in the late evening sunshine. She had realised suddenly, and with startling clarity, that she needed to face up to the past if she was ever going to move on.

It was also obvious to her now that several of her former colleagues felt that she had let them down by staying away for so long.

She stopped to watch a moorhen weaving in and out of the rushes and then she saw Ross approaching her from the other side of the lake. Her immediate reaction was to pretend that she hadn't seen him and retreat, but she realised it was too late. A few moments later he had caught up with her.

'You're not running away again, Annis?' he asked.

'Of course not. I'm just reflecting on a few things, that's all.'

'Well, you've certainly proved your worth today. Lisa and the others can't sing your praises enough. It's a pity you didn't tell Stella I'd agreed to you working in the kitchen, though. It would have saved her a bit of embarrassment.'

'I can't imagine Stella being embarrassed about anything,' Annis said, staring at him coldly. 'In any case, why did she feel the need to interfere with what was going on in the kitchen? When I worked here previously, everyone ran their own department, with Bryn and Arnie at the helm. Everyone respected what everyone else did, and didn't interfere.'

Ross's eyes glinted. 'Things have changed since you were here last, Annis, and the sooner you realise that the better. We can't put the clock back, so we just have to move on. Stella has been a pillar of support during these past few months. She's my right-hand woman. Sadly, since the accident Bryn hasn't been able to take such an active part as he used to do.'

'So you go off and make all the

decisions and present them to him as a *fait accompli*?'

'You're determined to see me in a bad light, aren't you?' He sighed. 'We all try not to put him under too much pressure, but as you're fully aware, he still has the final say.'

'For the moment, at any rate,' she countered, and met his angry gaze.

He cast a pebble into the lake, as if to gain control.

'Well, anyway, Sally will be back on Monday, so I guess you'll be heading back to London soon?'

Annis met his gaze levelly. 'There's no particular rush. I've got another week's leave, and I don't suppose Chef will be back for at least a week.'

'No, but we've got someone coming from the agency on Tuesday and our sous chef will be back by then, too. I've been to see Niall. He's been under a lot of pressure recently and the doctor's signed him off for a couple of weeks, but his wife will be back in a few days. Our sous chef will naturally take charge once he's here, but if Sally or yourself can be spared until he gets back, then we'd obviously be grateful for your help.'

'Of course.' Annis thought for a moment, and then she told Ross, 'Coming here has made me do a lot of thinking about my situation.'

'So you didn't come merely to visit Sally and Bryn?'

'At first, yes, but now I've taken a long, hard look at myself and I realise that it's high time I let go of the past. I've told Bryn I'd like to come back permanently.'

There was a laden silence.

'I see,' he said at last. 'You're full of surprises, aren't you? Ever since you've been here, you've made it painfully clear that you disapprove of most of the changes. And yet . . . '

She folded her arms. 'Yes, well, in the past we all pulled together and relationships were good. I've been on a few team-building courses while I've been working in London, and I suppose

I must have learned something.'

To her surprise, he nodded. 'I'll admit there have been a few problems recently, but this is a business and . . . '

'There's no sentiment in business!' she finished, echoing the phrase she had heard him use before. 'You know, you're in danger of losing the caring atmosphere that made this place what it was. You'll get far more work out of the staff if they're happy in their environment and know that they're valued.'

He fell silent once more, and she wondered if she had gone too far. But he appeared to be mulling her words over in his mind.

'You've had your say, so now let me have mine. You've stated that you want to let go of the past — fine. But in doing so, you'll have to be prepared to accept the changes. We do things differently now and there's no going back. We've got to move forward, however hard it may be for you.' He looked levelly at her. 'Personally I'm not at all sure that you're suited to the present way of working.'

Annis gaped at him, unable to believe her ears.

'I've worked my socks off for the past fortnight in order to prove to you and Tristan that I can make a valuable contribution to the workforce!'

'Yes, I don't deny that, but you've also got to prove that you're prepared to work as part of this new regime, and I'm not sure that you are. Anyway, we've both had a long day. Think about what I've said. I'm going to have a drink in the bar before turning in — care to join me?'

She bit back an angry retort.

'Another time, perhaps. I've got an early start in the morning.'

Annis went to her room and off to bed with a heavy heart.

Lunch With Bryn

On Sunday, Annis got up early and lent a hand with the breakfasts. Lisa's sister, April, had arrived to help out, and everything was nicely under control. Lisa said that they could manage until around four o'clock, so, when Bryn asked if she would like to accompany him and Ross to church that morning, Annis accepted, determined to put her differences with Ross aside.

The Norman church was beautifully cool, and sun streamed through the stained glass windows creating dancing rainbow patterns on the floor. It was a lovely service and afterwards they went up to Andrew's grave for a few moments, and placed some fresh flowers.

As Ross drove them home, Bryn said, 'We'll have coffee in the garden this morning. Tristan's on the desk and

Vicki's offered to do a stint in the kitchen, so you'll have no excuses, either of you.'

Ross went off to rustle up some coffee, and Annis escorted Bryn into the garden and settled him on a comfortable seat beneath an arbour of roses.

'So, what do you reckon to the garden, Annis? Like it, do you?'

'It's beautiful — John's done an amazing job.'

'It's a quiet sanctuary after a busy day's work. We're planning to have a fountain here, in memory of Andrew.'

'He would have liked that,' Annis said quietly.

Presently, Ross returned with the coffee and, sitting in the peaceful surroundings of the garden with the bees droning in and out of the lavender, she could almost forget what Ross had said to her the previous day. He was looking very relaxed that morning and was very attentive to Bryn's needs.

For the next half-hour or so, they

discussed village activities and the next project that John had in mind for the garden. When Annis got to her feet, saying that she would go and see if they needed any help in the kitchen over lunchtime, Bryn insisted that she sat down again.

'Annis, I've told you, it's all sorted! Tristan is doing a turn on reception and Vicki's lending a hand in the kitchen. Both you and Ross need some off-duty time, and I'm going to see that you get it.'

Ross and Annis exchanged looks.

'You're both coming out to lunch with me,' Bryn announced. 'It's all arranged. I've booked a table at 'The Chestnut Tree'.'

Ross winked at Annis and she smiled back, knowing from past experience that it would be useless to argue with Bryn, for he was a very determined character.

To get to 'The Chestnut Tree' they drove along winding country lanes, past hedgerows starred with dog roses, until they reached the restaurant, which nestled on the outskirts of a village not far from where Sally's parents lived.

It was a delightful meal in a pleasant environment and Ross was at his most charming. Annis couldn't help wondering if Bryn had an ulterior motive in inviting both of them.

Presently, he set down his knife and fork and sighed with satisfaction.

'That was a good roast. I shall send my compliments to the chef.'

Over dessert he said, 'So, now that you've been here for a while Annis, have you come up with any explanation for all the problems Sally's been experiencing of late? It's not like her to be careless.'

Annis was aware that Ross was watching her keenly, but she had to be honest.

'I only wish I could give you an answer, but I'm afraid I can't at present, except that I don't believe Sally is to blame. She's far too efficient. So perhaps we should be looking elsewhere.'

Ross frowned and Bryn raised his hand. 'OK, we'll leave it for now. It doesn't look as if we're going to get to the bottom of the matter in five minutes. Let's just hope Sally returns from her course with her batteries recharged. And now that Annis is soon to replace Zoe, albeit on a temporary basis to begin with, then Sally won't feel under so much pressure. So, who's for coffee?'

Annis shot a look at Ross and saw that his mouth was set in a grim line. He had made it clear that he wasn't exactly ecstatic about her appointment and she knew that she would have her work cut out to prove herself.

'By the way, before I forget, I'm coming to sit in on one of the client interviews tomorrow morning, Annis,' Bryn told her. 'I thought I'd take up your suggestion and become more involved.'

'That's really good news, Bryn,' she said, smiling at him.

* * *

Back at the Mill, Ross followed Annis out into the garden.

'I don't know about you but after that lunch I could do with a spot of exercise before going back on duty,' he said. 'Fancy a game of tennis?'

Taken by surprise, she found herself agreeing and hurried off to change into shorts and T-shirt. She tied her hair back with a piece of ribbon and went along to the courts where Ross was waiting for her, swinging a couple of racquets.

He looked even more attractive in his white shorts and T-shirt, which showed off his tan to advantage.

He was good at tennis. They had the courts to themselves and Annis found herself enjoying his company more than she had expected. If only it could always be like this.

The time went by quickly, and it was almost four o'clock before she realised it.

As they came off the court, Stella came out from reception looking extremely glamorous in a jade coloured dress, her dark curls beautifully styled. Beside her, Annis felt sticky and untidy.

'Ah, there you are, Ross! I thought we could go for a drive out into the country. It's far too nice a day to be stuck indoors.'

Ross gave her a charming smile. 'Sorry, Stella, but I'm just about to go back on duty.'

Stella looked sulky and took his arm. 'Can't you swap with Tristan?'

Ross shook his head. 'No, sorry. Some other time maybe?' And he strode away towards the staff quarters, leaving Annis and Stella standing.

Stella turned to smile coolly at Annis. 'Ross is an absolute darling — so considerate of others — but he's also something of a workaholic. One word of warning, Annis — he's not a bit like Andrew, except in looks, of course.'

Annis murmured something about going to the kitchen and walked away, wondering what message Stella was trying to convey. Was she trying to warn her off? Well, she needn't worry: Annis had no intention of getting involved with Andrew's cousin, even though her emotions were inexplicably in turmoil.

* * *

On Monday morning, Annis was busy with breakfasts for the conference delegates when Tristan put in an appearance in the kitchen.

'So, this is where you've been hiding! I wondered where you'd got to this morning, Annis. How are things?'

'Fine,' she told him briskly. 'Everything's under control, isn't it, Lisa?'

Lisa nodded and went on serving up bacon and eggs.

'Good, then I'll leave you to it. Are you here all morning, Annis?'

'No, I'm going over to the office shortly. Sally should be in just before nine.'

But Sally was already in the office

when Annis got there.

'How was the course?' Annis asked her.

'Brilliant! I feel like a new woman.' Sally grinned. 'Thanks for holding the fort. How's it been?'

'Everything went according to plan — no hitches.'

'Well, I'm glad about that, but — ' Sally looked doubtful ' — doesn't that prove that I'm the one who's making all the mistakes?'

'How do you work that out? We'll just have to hope things go more smoothly from now on and be extra vigilant about spotting mistakes before they get into the system. Anyway, there have been plenty of problems in other directions — so brace yourself.'

Annis told her about the problems in the kitchen.

'Oh, poor Chef — and poor Niall. I thought he'd been looking under a bit of strain recently. Stella's pretty good at putting her foot in it. Anyway, it just goes to show what a decent lot they are here, all being prepared to rally round like that.'

'Yes, but that's how it ought to be all of the time,' Annis pointed out.

Sally was looking through the appointments book.

'You know, I enjoyed that course so much! It restored some of my confidence, and I began to think that if it wasn't for Uncle Bryn I'd leave here — apply for a job elsewhere.'

Annis stared at her, knowing that she must persuade her not to take such a drastic step.

'Sally, don't you dare leave — not when I've just packed in my London job so that I can come back here.'

Sally gave a whoop of delight and hugged her friend.

'That's the best news I've heard in a long time! Things are certainly looking up!'

'Oh, and I nearly forgot: Bryn's coming down to sit in on the client interviews this morning,' Annis informed her. 'I told you I'd suggested he should get more involved.'

'Well, you've certainly achieved results since I've been away,' Sally said admiringly.

'I'm doing my best. How do you fancy a stint in the kitchen while I do the second interview?'

Sally beamed at her. 'I'd love to — you know how I like cooking.'

'And if we share the interviews and anything goes wrong in the future, then we can share the blame, too!' Annis teased.

Sally pulled a face. 'Don't say that! I'm just hoping everything's sorted itself out.'

* * *

Bryn appeared in the office just before ten o'clock. The first clients were a rather nervous-looking girl and her mother. The girl was obviously under her mother's thumb, and Annis and Sally had to coax her to say what she really wanted — while being continually interrupted by her mother, who wanted to have everything her own way.

It required a great deal of tact and diplomacy to handle them, and after they'd departed an hour and a quarter later, Bryn congratulated both Sally and Annis on the way they'd dealt with the situation.

He expressed a wish to go over to the boutique to see Madame Cecile, and, since the next clients weren't due to arrive for another hour, Annis volunteered to go with him, while Sally escaped to the kitchen.

Bryn leaned heavily on Annis's arm as they walked across the grass.

'It was a good idea of yours to get me more involved, Annis. I was turning into a bit of an old stick-in-the-mud up there in my flat.'

'Well, it's far too nice a day to be indoors,' Annis told him.

Madame Cecile looked up and smiled as they entered the boutique.

'Mr Freeman, how delightful to see you — and Miss Fuller, too.'

Annis sat down out of the way while Bryn and Madame Cecile sat near the front counter, deep in conversation, bent over the order book.

Annis took the opportunity to look about her. It was an attractive little shop, tastefully furnished. In a corner of the room, Lara sat stitching away, wearing a perpetual frown.

Annis observed her while pretending to look at a glossy magazine, but suddenly the woman glanced up and met her gaze, and Annis was startled by the bleak misery in her eyes.

Perhaps she had an unhappy home life, Annis speculated, and on impulse crossed to Lara's side and bent to examine the gown she was working on.

'That's beautiful, Lara. You really are gifted.'

Just for a moment, the woman's face softened.

'Thank you, Miss Fuller, but I can't take all the credit — Madame does so much of the work herself.'

Overhearing, Madame Cecile looked

across at them. 'Lara is too modest. We all play an important part. We aim to satisfy our customers.'

Millie came rushing in just as Annis and Bryn were about to leave the shop later. Her face lit up when she saw the old man.

'Hello, Millie of Heathercote Mill,' he quipped.

'Uncle Bryn, what are you doing here?'

'Camille!' her mother chided, frowning sternly at her daughter's familiar tone.

'I thought it was about time I paid you all a visit. How's life in the kitchen?' Bryn asked Millie, smiling at her indulgently.

'Oh, busy as usual, Uncle Bryn!' said Millie, smiling back at him.

'Camille, now that you're here, you can make yourself useful and sew on some sequins,' her mother said sharply. 'Lara needs a break.'

Millie picked up some sequins that had fallen to the floor.

'Oh, all right, but I can only spare an hour . . . I've got a rehearsal this evening and I need to practice my dance.'

As they made their way back to the Mill, Bryn said, 'That girl is going to rebel if Cecile pushes her too hard.'

'Mm,' Annis agreed. 'But I don't see what we can do about it.'

'We'll just have to think of something, won't we?' The old gentleman winked at her. 'It's obvious to everyone — apart from her mother — that her heart isn't in the dressmaking business. Now, let's stop here for a few minutes so that I can get my breath back.'

He sank down thankfully on to the bench he had indicated and patted the space beside him. Annis still had around ten minutes before her next interview, so she was content to sit down too.

'I told you Cecile and I are sort of related, didn't I?' said Bryn.

Annis nodded. 'You said Madame Cecile was married to your wife's

. . . cousin's son, was it?'

'That's it exactly. Well, Madame Cecile's husband died in a boating accident in France a couple of years ago, so she decided to make a fresh start in England. She wrote to me to see if there was any work she could do, and at my invitation she came to see me, bringing Millie with her. Cecile is fiercely independent and I . . . '

'You created the job for her?'

'Actually, yes, I did.' He smiled. 'It wasn't the first time Arnold or I had done such a thing, and I'm sure it won't be the last. She'd fallen on hard times. Without betraying any confidences, I'll just say that — well, to put it mildly, it seems her husband wasn't very good with money. She only just managed to scrape together enough for her fare over here.'

He paused and offered Annis a mint.

'Oh, I know I took a chance, but I think you'll agree that she's an excellent dressmaker, conscientious and hard-working, and she's bringing a lot of extra trade to the Mill — and Millie's a delightful girl.'

'She certainly is. Where do they live?' Annis unwrapped her mint.

'Oh, I own a couple of cottages in the village and they rent one of those. Changing the subject, it's a pity that her assistant, Lara, looks so miserable. You wouldn't believe young Vicki on reception is her daughter, would you? Of course, now I come to think of it, it was Vicki's younger sister who worked for Sally for a short while. Did Sally tell you about that?'

'Yes, she did,' Annis said cautiously, not sure how much he knew about the girl's behaviour.

'Oh, it's all right, lass, I'm aware that she made life difficult for Sally — not much escapes my notice!'

'I'm sure it doesn't, Bryn.'

'I've been keeping too much of a low profile recently and now I need to make my presence felt — you've made me see that.' He sucked on his mint. 'Anyway, I'm aware that there have been a number of problems recently. It makes me sad to know that things aren't right. I think of my employees as my extended family, as you know, and when there's discord, it grieves me.

'I know that Ross is a good fellow, but at the end of the day, I'm the one at the helm and the only one who can really sort matters out. I sit up there in my room and I think of the old times with Arnie, Andrew and you, Annis — the three A's — and of how things used to be.'

'Is that why you've taken to staying up in your flat? Because things have been a bit difficult down here?' she asked him gently.

He nodded, and she squeezed his hand.

'Anyway, you've come back now, Annis, and you don't know how much that means to me. But enough of all this. There's work to be done!'

Annis helped him to his feet and they went across to the Mill.

He'd given her a lot of food for thought.

* * *

After a busy day, Sally and Annis were tidying up the office when Tristan wandered in, apparently looking for a chat.

'How did you enjoy the course, Sally?'

'Very much! Thanks for letting me go, Tristan — I owe you one.'

'No problem — I'm glad that you found it worthwhile. Anyway, what I really came to ask was whether you'd like a trip out this evening, Annis? Just a pub meal — maybe a club if you're up for it? I gather you're going away at the end of the week, so this will probably be the last opportunity I've got to wine and dine you.'

'I'll be back again next weekend . . . ' she pointed out.

'No can do, I'm afraid. I've swapped with Ross so that I can take Stella to see our mother — lots of things to discuss.'

Annis would have preferred to have stayed in that evening, but Tristan was persuasive and she found herself accepting his invitation.

'You seem to be getting on well with Tristan,' Sally remarked when he'd gone.

'Don't read too much into it, Sally. Remember what I said when I first came here? I want to keep in with both Ross and Tristan so that I can find out about any future plans for the Mill. But I do find Tristan good company, as it happens.'

'Oh, he can charm a bird off a tree, but don't get too involved, will you? He likes to play the field, and I wouldn't like to see you getting hurt.'

'I can take care of myself, Sally,' Annis told her rather sharply.

'Oh, well, it's your life,' Sally said.

That evening, Annis barely had time to shower and change into a cotton skirt and top before meeting up with Tristan.

'You look nice,' he said. 'I've booked a table at a place I know in the country.'

As he drove, he kept up a light, bantering chatter for a time, but then he suddenly became more serious.

'Ross says you're considering joining us permanently. It would be good to have your smiling face about the place. I don't know if you've picked up on the vibes, but the Mill's not always the happiest of places these days. I'm afraid quite a bit of backbiting goes on.'

'Well, things are bound to get fraught from time to time,' Annis said, choosing her words carefully and wondering whether she would be able to glean any useful information from this conversation. 'Staff morale does seem a bit low, and staff-turnover seems to be quite high,' she commented.

Noticing the rather annoyed expression that flitted across Tristan's face, she added, 'I'm only making an observation.'

'You seem to have made quite a few

in the short time you've been here,' he said abruptly, and she found herself colouring. 'So tell me, Annis, what would you do to make things right?'

She swallowed, feeling trapped, and wished she hadn't started this.

'Well, years ago, each department worked happily without members of management staff feeling the need to interfere every five minutes,' she ventured. 'There doesn't seem to be much trust nowadays and it undermines staff confidence.'

'Oh, come on, Annis! When I arrived here, it needed someone at the helm. Obviously Bryn isn't up to it nowadays, so all of us managers work it between us.'

'And cause resentment in certain areas whilst you're at it?' she asked.

She knew she had gone too far. His knuckles on the wheel were white and he shot her a glance from blazing eyes.

'So, what would you do then? You must see that now that the Mill enterprises have grown so big, we need people with management skills to co-ordinate things. We can't have everyone doing their own thing or we'd never get anywhere.'

Annis took a deep breath. 'Yes, I can see that, but I'd choose a representative from each department to attend staff meetings. That way, no-one could complain that they hadn't been given a fair opportunity to express their opinions.'

He pulled up outside an attractive pub decorated with hanging baskets of trailing petunias and lobelia, and Annis was relieved that the conversation had been put on hold, at least for the time being.

It was still warm enough to eat outside and, after ordering their food, they took their drinks and sat in the last of the evening sunshine, looking out over a magnificent view of the weald of Kent.

'So, tell me more about what you've been doing during the past few years,' Tristan asked, after some general chat.

'I know you work in London, but have you been there ever since you left here?'

'No, I spent the first eighteen months or so in Dorset, staying with my parents and working in one of the local hotels. Then I went on a couple of training courses. I also spent about six weeks visiting friends in America.'

'So, you've actually only been in London for around three years?'

'About that, yes.' She sipped her drink, wondering where the conversation was leading.

'So, why do you want to come back here? Why now?'

'It's too hot in London during the summer,' she said, and he laughed.

'That's hardly a strong enough reason for leaving a perfectly good job to return to the Mill in a temporary capacity — presumably on a lower rate of pay. Unless, of course, you've had another broken relationship.'

She stared at him.

'I'm here because I've missed the

buzz of 'Something Borrowed, Something Blue' and I've missed my friends,' she said vehemently. 'I had a lot of leave accrued — through working flexi-hours — so I thought it would be a good opportunity to spend some time with Sally and John, and also to lend Sally a hand.'

'Well, it's a funny sort of holiday.'

'Not at all. Being here *is* like a holiday — lovely countryside, good company, and a pleasant environment at the Mill. I've no food to cook and my room's cleaned for me — what more could I ask for?'

Tristan didn't look convinced.

'But you don't honestly think you can turn up here and carry on where you left off almost five years ago? You can't be that naive.'

She coloured. 'Of course not — I realise that we have to move on and there have to be changes.'

Fortunately, the food arrived just then. It looked delicious, but Annis felt bemused by what Tristan had just said.

He was so full of contrasts and tonight she felt she was seeing a different side to his character.

She tried to concentrate on her meal, although suddenly it tasted like cardboard in her mouth.

First Ross, and now Tristan — both obviously trying to trap her into admitting that she had an ulterior motive in visiting the Mill.

Much to her relief, Tristan dropped the subject and became his former amusing self, telling her about a film that he'd seen the previous week.

'With Vicki?' she asked casually.

'Yes, it was, as a matter of fact.' He gave a little laugh.

Annis suddenly thought of something. 'Tristan, I've been wondering — Vicki's mother, Lara, doesn't seem at all happy. Do you know of any problem?'

Tristan hesitated. 'Well, I don't suppose it matters if I tell you,' he said. 'It's hardly a state secret. Her daughter's left home.'

'Kelly?'

'Yes. She's always been a bit of a problem kid, and after packing in her job at the Mill, she just upped and went off to Spain with some mates. She's OK — Vicki's had a couple of e-mails — but she's not letting on exactly where she's staying. She's having a whale of a time, apparently. But Lara's worried sick.'

So that explained why the poor woman looked so pale and drawn.

'Oh, poor Lara. How old is Kelly?'

'About eighteen — grown up and yet not so grown up, if you see what I mean.'

The rest of the evening passed pleasantly enough, but Annis declined Tristan's offer to go to a night club, saying that she had a busy day ahead of her on Tuesday. Bryn was holding a staff meeting in the morning, and he'd insisted that Sally took the rest of the day off while Annis was still there to cover.

* * *

The next day was as hectic as Annis had anticipated. There was one wedding on the Thursday of that week, two on the Friday and three on the Saturday, so there was plenty to keep her occupied. To her surprise, Bryn was adamant that she took Wednesday off and that she came to dinner with him and the others on Thursday evening.

She ran into Ross at lunch. 'Ah, the very person I wanted to see,' he greeted her. 'I was wondering if you could do me a favour? It's your day off tomorrow, isn't it?'

'Yes. Do you want me to change it?'

'What are you planning to do?'

'Catch up on a few chores — laundry, letters, shopping.'

'What an exciting life you lead!' He laughed. 'How would it be if you took me to Leeds Castle instead? I've never been there and it's not much fun going alone.'

She stared at him in amazement, wondering if he was serious.

'I take it you *have* been there before?' he asked.

'Bryn took Sally and I when we were about fourteen. I don't think I appreciated it back then.'

'OK, so how about I pick you up around ten-thirty?'

Annis felt her heart pounding. A whole day out with Ross Hadley!

* * *

Next morning, Annis ran into Stella on her way out of the dining-room. 'Ross tells me you're off out this morning,' Stella said. 'We were going to have lunch together, but I've had to change my time off because I'm away this weekend. Enjoy yourself.'

She gave a wistful little smile, watching for Annis's reaction. Annis felt furious, not so much with Stella but with Ross. Then she reminded herself that he had been friends with Stella for many years — and she was even crosser with herself for minding so much.

She managed a quick trip into Heronsbridge for some shopping and to go to the bank, and was just about ready by half past ten.

Ross was already waiting in the Mercedes, and he opened the door for her.

As she fastened her seat-belt she said, casually, 'I saw Stella earlier. I gather she's had to change her off-duty time.'

'Oh, yes, Tris and Stella are away for the weekend. She's got plenty to keep her occupied whilst I'm out. How are you two getting along?'

'Oh, fine. We don't see much of each other, and when we do, we're perfectly civil — after all, life has to go on.' She hoped she sounded convincing.

They were driving along a narrow country lane bordered by woodland. The trees formed a canopy overhead and the sunlight trickled through, dappling the leaves. She sighed with pleasure and he shot her a swift glance.

'That was heartfelt.'

'I was just thinking how much I've

missed all this. Kent is such a beautiful county.'

'So I'm discovering.'

They rounded a corner and came upon a cluster of cottages and, in the background, an oast house set against a backdrop of rolling countryside. It was a beautiful drive and Annis found herself enjoying every minute of it. Presently, they arrived at the entrance to the castle.

'I know that Leeds Castle has the reputation of being the most beautiful castle in the world, but not much else about it,' Ross said.

'Well, I've been reading up about it,' Annis informed him. 'It's listed in the Domesday Book, and dates back to Saxon times, but the buildings you'll see go back to the Normans. Its last private owner was Lady Baillie, and she's to be thanked for its restoration.'

The castle, standing on two islands in a lake, was stunningly beautiful. Annis glanced at Ross to see his reaction. He stood in silence for a while.

'It's magnificent,' he said at last. 'I've always had a thing about castles, ever since I was a child. There's so much to see here that I don't know where to begin.'

They had a wonderful day. Ross was a charming companion and Annis couldn't remember the last time she'd enjoyed herself so much.

They did a mixture of things, from watching the famous black swans on the lake, to wandering through the delightful parkland. They lunched in the terrace restaurant and talked on a variety of subjects until, over coffee, he steered the conversation round to her plans for the future.

'I have no immediate plans other than filling in for Zoe on a temporary basis,' she told him 'I'll just take each day as it comes and see how things work out.'

'Annis, since you've been here, Bryn has taken on a new lease of life. We've all been so busy with our own areas of work that we've been neglecting him recently, but now he's taking so much more interest in the Mill that he's keeping us on our toes. He's already pinpointed a few things that need sorting out.'

'You can learn a lot from Bryn Freeman,' she told him. 'He's a very wise gentleman. He just needed to feel useful again, rather than being a mere figurehead who signs all the cheques and important letters.'

'We thought we were doing the right thing in keeping any problems away from him.' Ross sighed. 'But now I can see that we might have been overprotective.'

'The Mill is Bryn's lifeblood now that Arnold and Andrew have gone,' Annis told him. 'I see now that I ought to have returned long ago and I realise I've been very selfish,' Annis admitted quietly.

'We all have, Annis. We've all been pulling in different directions, wanting what was best for ourselves and not thinking about others. Anyway, all that's going to change from now on.' He got to his feet. 'We'll continue this discussion another time. Right now, I want to see the inside of this castle.'

They wandered around the interior of the castle admiring the antiques, tapestries and paintings and then, coming out once more into the brilliant sunshine, they walked down to the castle vineyard. Finally, they went into the maze and, finding that they were alone, Ross drew her to him and kissed her gently.

'Thank you, Annis — it's been a lovely day.'

Annis's heart was doing strange things. 'I've enjoyed it too, Ross, so thank *you*,' she said, rather unsteadily.

He caught her hand as they wandered back through the grounds.

'We must come here again sometime, Annis. Hopefully you and I are going to be good friends from now on.'

She smiled up at him and murmured, 'I do hope so, Ross.'

The Mystery Is Solved

The rest of the week flew past. Sally and Annis were incredibly busy with all the weddings but fortunately the agency chef had turned out to be a treasure. Sunday morning came round all too quickly and John took Annis to the station.

'I can't thank you enough, Annis,' he said, planting a kiss on her cheek. 'Sally is so much more her old self and her confidence is returning. Going on that course was just what she needed.'

'I'm glad to have been of help, John. I think Sally needed to know that people had faith in her. Hopefully everything will run smoothly from now on.'

As she sat on the train heading towards London, Annis thought over the events of the past few days. The weddings had been all that anyone could have wished for. There had been no major disasters, only one or two minor hitches that couldn't have been prevented.

She smiled as she remembered them. On Thursday, a bridesmaid had caught her foot in the hem of the bride's dress and torn it. Fortunately, Madame Cecile had been on hand to do an expert repair job.

On Friday, one of the small pageboys had been distraught at the loss of his teddy bear. Dean had found it mysteriously wedged under one of the tables, and Millie had gone into gales of laughter at the sight of him, down on all fours, retrieving the much-loved toy.

On Saturday, the best man at one wedding had had an unfortunate encounter with a glass of red wine and ruined his waistcoat, and the bride's mother at one of the other weddings had lost her hat in the lake. Annis giggled at the memory and pulled herself together when she realised that the rather stern-looking woman sitting opposite was frowning at her over her newspaper.

Millie had been upset when she'd learned that Annis was going away, but had brightened when she'd realised that she'd be back over the bank holiday weekend to see the play.

When Annis had gone up to say goodbye to Bryn, he had embraced her warmly.

'This is going to seem a long week without you, Annis — roll on Friday!' he'd said.

Ross had been deep in conversation with Vicki when Annis had been ready to leave, but he'd looked up briefly.

'I look forward to our next meeting, Annis — have a safe journey and a good week.'

She felt a warm glow inside her as she thought about Ross's kiss. She knew that she would miss him, and wondered how she would get through the week ahead.

Much to her surprise, her time in London went by quickly. Now that she'd given in her notice, her boss seemed charm itself and Fiona, who was replacing her, actually asked her advice on a few matters. The job that Annis was doing was rather mundane, but because she was looking forward to returning to Heathercote Mill at the end of the week, she didn't mind.

Her friends at the flat, while sorry that she was leaving, weren't unduly worried about finding someone else to share. They had all thought she was mad to spend her entire holiday working, and couldn't believe it when she told them her plans for the next month.

She had brought back a virtually empty case so that she could fill it with more of her possessions, and spent most of her free time packing up, but she still managed to go out with friends to the cinema one evening.

Sally phoned her a couple of times, telling her that everything was still going well. Annis just hoped that this would continue to be the case; she still couldn't believe that Sally had been responsible for the mistakes that had occurred, but she was unable to come up with any logical explanation.

* * *

When she stepped off the train on Friday afternoon, Annis met up with three wedding guests who were bound for the Mill, and they invited her to share a cab with them. As soon as she had been to her room to leave her luggage and tidy herself up, she made her way to the office, to be greeted by a beaming Sally.

'I've had the best week ever, Annis — even the rain on Wednesday couldn't dampen my spirits. But now the next ceremony kicks off in around half an hour and one of the bridesmaids has managed to lose her headdress. Don't ask! Her mother thinks it was deliberate because the child took a dislike to it. Anyway, it came from here and Madame Cecile says she's got one in stock the right size, so could you be an angel and go and collect it? Lara was going to bring it over but she's cutting it a bit fine.'

Annis sped down to the boutique and was surprised to find Madame Cecile looking a little flustered.

'How nice to see you, Miss Fuller . . . I'm afraid I had completely forgotten about the headdress.' She lowered her voice. 'There has been a bit of a problem here.'

Annis could see Lara sitting in the corner dabbing her eyes.

'What's wrong?' she whispered. 'Is it anything I can help with?'

Madame Cecile shook her head and ushered Annis into the storeroom.

'Today is her daughter, Kelly's, birthday and Lara does not know how to get in touch with her. She's in Spain, but has given no address. She is a wilful girl, Miss Fuller. When she was here she caused trouble for us . . . '

'What kind of trouble?' Annis asked, but Madame Cecile obviously felt that she had said enough.

'It is over now, but Lara misses her

daughter so much, it makes her unhappy.'

Fortunately, Madame Cecile found the headdress just then, and Annis hurried back with it, just in time for it to be placed on the protesting bridesmaid's head.

'Thank goodness for that!' Sally exclaimed. 'Annis, you must be gasping for a cuppa. Come and get one now, before something else crops up.'

The wedding ceremony and reception went off without any further hitches and, much later, as they sat over supper cooked by John, Annis relayed what had happened at the boutique earlier.

'That woman looks sour enough to curdle the milk,' John commented.

'Oh, poor Lara — you know, now I come to think of it, there was an incident at the boutique concerning Kelly, but it was all hushed up.'

Annis was thoughtful. She wondered whether Madame Cecile might be persuaded to tell her exactly what had happened.

She went over to the boutique straight after breakfast. Madame Cecile was already at work, completing a bridesmaid's dress, and although pleasant enough, she was disinclined to chatter. In answer to Annis's enquiry after Lara, she merely said, 'Oh, she is quite all right now. Vicki had an e-mail from her sister last night. It seems she plans to stay in Spain for a while longer. She has found herself a job in a bar.'

'Madame, you mentioned some trouble — what happened?' Annis asked carefully.

Madame Cecile laid aside her sewing. 'It would be disloyal of me to say, Miss Fuller. It is water under the bridge now, as you say. At the time it was upsetting, but now it is forgotten.' She looked directly at Annis. 'Mr Hadley dealt with the situation.'

After a few remarks about the weather, Annis took her leave. Her mind was buzzing with lots of disconnected thoughts, but she was kept far too busy for the rest of the day to dwell on them much.

The weddings were a triumph, and Sally was in a state of euphoria at the end of them. The second reception wound up at about eleven o'clock and Annis went thankfully to bed.

* * *

She was up with the lark the next morning, and went for an early swim where, coming out of the changing rooms, she encountered Ross.

'I was beginning to think you were avoiding me,' he said.

'Why would I do that? Things were a bit hectic yesterday, that's all.'

They enjoyed their swim, but it wasn't long before he had to go.

'Work beckons,' he said. 'We're like ships that pass in the night, aren't we? I'm off at eight, though — how about coming out for a meal with me?'

Annis's heartbeat quickened as he smiled at her.

'I'd enjoy that, Ross.'

'Great — I'll see you in the bar.'

Annis enjoyed a pleasant, relaxing day. She went to church with Sally, John, and Bryn, and then Bryn insisted on her joining him for lunch in his flat. She spent the rest of the afternoon reading in the staff garden.

That evening, she showered and selected a pink and cream cotton dress, glad that she had brought some more clothes back with her. She applied her make up carefully, leaving her newly-washed hair to fall in a shining curtain about her shoulders.

She arrived in the bar before Ross, and exchanged a few words with Dean, Millie's boyfriend. After a few minutes, Ross came in and Annis watched him as he stopped to talk to a couple of the staff. He was wearing a pale blue, open-necked shirt and dark blue trousers. His chestnut hair fell forward over his forehead, making him look boyish. He spotted her and raised his hand in greeting.

As they left the bar, Stella came through the swing doors. Her face lit up when she saw Ross, but she totally ignored Annis.

'Hello, Ross — are you off duty now? How about having a drink with me?'

'Another time, Stella. I'm taking Annis out to dinner. I'll catch up with you tomorrow and you can tell me all about your weekend.'

'I was hoping to tell you now, but never mind,' Stella said ungraciously.

Annis saw the expression on her face and realised that she saw Annis as a potential threat. She gave Stella what she hoped was a friendly smile, but Stella turned on her heel and went back the way she had come.

'She's got a lot on her mind at the moment,' Ross said, to ease an awkward moment, and Annis decided not to let Stella spoil the evening for her.

They drove along winding narrow lanes edged with cow parsley and poppies. Sheep grazed peacefully in the meadows and for a little while Annis sat in silence enjoying the scenery. It wasn't until they passed through a village with a cluster of thatched-roofed cottages and a church spire in the background that she spoke.

'I was a bit apprehensive about returning to the Mill but now, in spite of the changes, it's beginning to feel as if I've never been away.'

'You've done wonders for Bryn,' he said. 'He's a new person. I haven't seen him so interested in things for a long time, and it's good for staff morale to see him about the place.'

'So you don't object to my taking over Zoe's job for the time being?'

'No. And now that I've got to know you a bit more and realise that you're genuinely interested in the future of the Mill, I think it would be good if you joined us on a more permanent basis.'

He pulled in at a hotel, almost hidden behind a canopy of trees. It was one she hadn't visited before, but Ross seemed to know his way around. It was a very opulent establishment with deep, dusky pink carpets, large gilt-framed mirrors and huge arrangements of hydrangeas on marble-topped tables.

Annis wondered if she were appropriately dressed but then realised that Ross was taking her into the brasserie rather than the main restaurant.

They enjoyed a relaxed meal, talking about their families and friends, and the places they had visited on holidays, and then finally, over coffee, the conversation turned back to Heathercote Mill.

'There's a lot of potential there, and sometimes I wonder if it's being utilised properly,' Ross commented. 'The wedding business is a growing concern and we certainly do well enough out of the conferences, but I think there's scope for other activities.'

'What sort of other activities?'

She stirred her coffee, wondering what he was about to say.

'Summer schools, group activities, that sort of thing perhaps. At the moment, we're all geared up for business conferences but not much else. What do you think?'

'I'm only working here in a voluntary role at present, so I'm not really in a position to air my views,' she pointed out. 'For what it's worth though, and strictly off the record, I'll make just one observation.'

'Go on,' he invited, eyeing her keenly, so that she wondered what was going through his mind.

'All right. There are oceans of events and activities that could be thought up for the summer months, but what about the winter? You can't expect to be continually hiring and firing staff, not if you want any form of continuity, and . . . '

He grinned. 'OK, point taken. You know, I reckon you'd be an asset to the company. You've got the sort of business brain it takes — just as Bryn said, although I have to say, I've taken some convincing. One day you'll be pretty good in the consultancy field.'

'Well, there's one sure thing, I've no intention of trying out a consultancy role unless I'm doing so in a professional capacity on your payroll!' she told him.

He smiled at her, and she felt her heartbeat quicken.

'I've enjoyed tonight, Annis,' he said. 'I realise our relationship got off to a rocky start, but you've proved your worth and I look forward to you joining the team next month.'

She sipped her coffee and reached for another chocolate mint. It would have been nice to believe that he had asked her out because he wanted to get to know her better as a person, and not just to run a few ideas past her, but she supposed she would have to accept that Stella was always there in the background.

To him, she was sure, she was just Andrew's ex-fiancé, and he probably still viewed her presence in Heronsbridge with a certain amount of suspicion. He had a very strong protective instinct towards both his uncle and Stella, and he obviously wanted the business to flourish. He wouldn't have any scruples about changing things if he thought they weren't bringing in sufficient revenue, Annis knew — and if that meant closing down any aspect of the Mill enterprise that was a lame duck, then that was what would happen. She did feel, however, that he would do things with Bryn's best interests at heart.

She peeled the silver foil from her mint and rolled it into a tight ball

Ross regarded her with some amusement.

'Why don't you just say what's on your mind, instead of taking it out on that metal foil?' he asked.

She met his gaze steadily.

'I suppose I was just wondering whether — with all these changes you're thinking about — 'Something Borrowed, Something Blue' continues to have a place? I mean, it takes up a lot of time and energy, and whilst weddings are on the agenda, not much else can be, can it? I mean, take the play, for instance — the Mill would be a wonderful venue for open air productions, but Saturdays are the most popular time for weddings and . . . '

He held up his hand, a slight smile curving his lips. 'Hold on, tell me what makes you think we would jeopardise the wedding enterprise in order to promote new ideas?'

'I just thought, perhaps you had other plans? Men aren't all that interested in weddings.'

'You're priceless, Annis Fuller, did you know that? Without the male population there would be no weddings.' He laughed. 'I don't know what I have to say or do to convince you, but 'Something Borrowed, Something Blue' is always going to be one of the most important features of Heathercote Mill Enterprises.'

She nodded, and realised that here was a golden opportunity to ask Ross if he knew what had happened at the boutique concerning Kelly.

Briefly, she told him what had

happened on Friday and the comment made by Madame Cecile.

'Hm — I think the least said about that little episode the better.'

'Ross, I'm not just asking out of curiosity.' She told him what was on her mind and he whistled.

'You think Kelly might have been behind all the problems that Sally's been having with the wedding business lately? I'd never thought of that. I suppose it's feasible, although I don't quite see how she could have done it. Well, I suppose there's no harm in telling you what happened — it's over and done with now.

'Kelly is rather immature and she'd fallen out with her parents because they refused to give her the money to go to Spain with her friends during the summer. She came to work at the Mill against her will, although we didn't realise that until afterwards. On the day that she left, she had an enormous show-down with her parents — her father's quite strict.'

'So, what happened?'

'When the boutique was closed she got in and spoiled one of the wedding dresses that Madame Cecile was working on — and she also ruined an entire box of headdresses.'

'How did they know it was her?' Annis asked.

'She left a note — otherwise we would have called the police. Vicki thinks that's the reason she won't come back.'

'Because she's ashamed of what she did, you mean?'

'No, she's unrepentant, but she is a little concerned about the consequences of her actions. Look, if your theory is right . . . '

Annis shook her head. 'I don't know, it's only a hunch, and if Vicki can't get in touch with her sister and the girl's not prepared to own up, then how will we ever know for sure?'

He looked thoughtful. 'Well, that might not be as difficult as you think. Leave it with me. I'll have a word with

Vicki.' He glanced at his watch. 'Now, I'm sorry, but I have to get back — I've an early start in the morning and I have at least an hour's paperwork to do before I turn in.'

'You're a bit of a workaholic, aren't you, Ross?'

She got to her feet and reached for her jacket. He helped her on with it and she was aware that his closeness disturbed her profoundly.

When they arrived back at the Mill he caught her hands between his.

'I've enjoyed this evening, Annis, and I hope it'll be the first of many more. I look forward to getting to know you and to spending more time with you.'

'Thanks for a lovely meal, Ross,' she said, and she couldn't trust herself to look at him.

* * *

The week in London dragged. Annis had to fill in for a colleague who was off sick, and the job she had to cover was extremely boring and uninvolved. She couldn't wait to get away on Friday, and she knew it wasn't just because she'd had a difficult week.

When Friday came, Annis flew out of the office on the stroke of five o'clock and ran all the way to the railway station.

It was raining when she got off the train but, fortunately, she just managed to catch the hourly bus into Heronsbridge.

To her surprise, Sally was sitting in the office with her feet up drinking a cup of tea and reading a newspaper. She looked up and greeted Annis with a smile, but Annis thought she seemed weary.

'What's this? I thought there was a wedding this afternoon? Don't tell me it's been cancelled.'

'Nope, just postponed. The groom and his best man and mates went on a stag night to remember in Amsterdam, and missed their flight back. They couldn't get back in time for the ceremony. I've spent the entire day re-organizing everything. Fortunately it was to be a church wedding and the vicar, bless him, has agreed to marry them straight after the morning service on Sunday. Hopefully everything's sorted now, apart from a few bemused guests that we've had to accommodate because they live too far away to do a double journey.'

They caught up with the rest of the week's happenings over more cups of tea and then Sally gave a gasp.

'Oh, I nearly forgot — I've got a message here from Ross, asking you to have a word with Vicki. I don't know what it's about.'

Vicki was on reception as usual. She looked a bit apprehensive when she saw Annis, and asked one of the other girls to cover for her on the desk. She and Annis went into the conference dining-room, which was empty, and sat down together at a table.

'Miss Fuller, I don't know what to say. Ross told me that you suspect my sister might be behind the problems with the wedding business.' Vicki hesitated, biting her lip.

'Well . . . one of her friends, Jason, has just come back from Spain. I know him quite well and I asked him about her. Apparently, Kelly's been quite open about what she did — she thinks it's a huge joke.

'Anyway, after some persuasion, Jason gave me her new phone number. Would you believe that she deliberately left her mobile behind when she went away? And she's been refusing point blank to speak to my parents when they've tried to contact her on her friends' phones!'

'So what did she say?' Annis asked impatiently.

'Well, she's working in a bar and wasn't at all pleased that Jason had given me her number. At first she didn't want to talk, but eventually I managed to get it out of her.

'She said she got bored working on the weddings so she switched things around a bit — changed something here and there, but didn't alter it on the computer. Apparently she made a few phone calls, too. And on one occasion, she changed the champagne order and then made sure that it was her who was around to sign for it — that sort of thing. The mistakes didn't come to light until after she'd left, because she only targeted weddings scheduled to take place once she'd gone. She says she only did it for a joke.'

'Some joke!' Annis commented.

Vicki stared at her miserably.

'She only owned up because I told her that if she didn't, I'd tell our father and he'd come out to Spain to fetch her back. Miss Fuller, I am so sorry — I honestly had no idea what she was up to.'

'You mustn't blame yourself, Vicki. Well, hopefully we've caught up with all the blips now. Poor Sally, she really thought it was all her fault. Will you come with me now to tell her what really happened?'

'Of course I will. It's the very least I can do. I'm so sorry about all of this, and my mother will be so upset. It's bad enough what happened in the boutique, without all this.'

'Vicki, I don't see why we need to tell your mother about the bother with the wedding arrangements. It's all been resolved now, and I feel sure Sally will feel the same. The most important thing is to persuade your sister to come home.'

Vicki went with Annis to Sally's office, and Sally listened in silence while she repeated the story.

'There are two things I don't understand about all of this,' Sally said. 'How did she do it, and why?'

'She waited until you were out of your office and then made subtle changes here and there to weddings which you'd already checked out, and which she knew she wouldn't be around for — a telephone call here, a fax there. It wasn't anything personal,' Vicki said desperately. 'She's a very silly girl, I'll grant you that, but what we didn't realise was that her boyfriend had dumped her shortly after she came to work here. Working on wedding arrangements was the last straw when she was going through such an emotional crisis.'

When Vicki had gone back to reception, Sally burst into tears.

'Come on, Sal,' Annis comforted her. 'It's all over now, and it must be a relief to know that you're in the clear. Everyone will be so pleased.'

'But that's just it, isn't it?' Sally sniffed. 'They really believed the mistakes were my fault. They didn't have enough faith in me.'

Annis didn't know how to reply to this, because she knew Sally was right.

'I had faith in you, Sally,' she said quietly. 'And you know, perhaps all that's happened hasn't been in vain. Maybe Kelly has done us a favour.'

Sally looked at her in astonishment. 'How do you work that out?'

'She's shown us that we all need to

work as a team, but above all that, that we need to trust one another. Now, I'm going over to see Ross.'

'You can't.' Sally reached for a tissue. 'He's taken a few days' leave and gone up north to see his family. He's taken Stella with him, which is just as well because she's been so preoccupied just lately that she's not much use here. Anyway, Ross will cheer her up — they're good friends. The change will do them both good.'

* * *

Annis went through the rest of the day in a daze. She had been so looking forward to seeing Ross again — and now he was away for the entire weekend. She shouldn't have been surprised that he had taken Stella with him, and realised now that she had allowed herself to become too attracted to him. She was in danger of getting hurt all over again.

'What's up, Annis?' asked Bryn when

she went to see him. 'You don't look your usual sunny self. Are we wearing you out already?'

She assured him that she was fine and, after telling him her week's news, decided to tell him about Kelly.

'Well, I suppose it shouldn't surprise me. That girl always has been a bit of a problem — never sticks at anything for five minutes, unlike her sister who's reliable and conscientious. Maybe Kelly felt she couldn't measure up to Vicki and so she rebelled. Anyway, thank goodness it's all out in the open.'

He looked thoughtful.

'If, as you say, Sally is feeling undervalued, then we must put our heads together and do something about it, mustn't we? She's a very esteemed member of my staff. Now, the next problem we've got is Madame Cecile. Millie still doesn't think she's coming to see the play, so what can we do about that? Any bright ideas?'

'I'll put my thinking cap on,' she promised.

They shared another pot of tea and played a couple of games of Scrabble before Annis went to her room to get ready for supper. Her heart was heavy, but she knew she had burnt her boats. In a fortnight's time she would be returning here for good, so she would just have to get used to seeing Ross and Stella together.

Sally was back to her normal cheerful self the next day. She had decided not to tell Lara what her daughter had done.

'You know, it explains why Kelly changed so rapidly. She was so enthusiastic when she first came here. Obviously her head was full of the glamour of weddings, but then when her boyfriend 'dumped' her, as Vicki put it, things changed and that was when she seemed to lose interest.

'Well, Lara's got enough worries and I don't see the point in giving her any more. Anyway, although we're still going to have to double-check each wedding even more carefully than usual for the next few weeks, I really think things are looking up for me at last.'

The two girls got down to the business of the day, feeling satisfied that things were running smoothly once more. Just to prove it, both the weddings went like clockwork, with no hitches.

On Sunday, everyone helped to prepare for that morning's wedding celebration. Soon after twelve o'clock the bride and groom arrived for the reception in a horse-drawn carriage, and, much to everyone's relief, everything went off without any further problems.

The bride was radiant, and the dress made by Madame Cecile was a sensation in white silk and lace. As the happy couple embraced, Annis felt a lump in her throat and wondered if she would ever make it up the aisle herself.

Once the wedding was over, Annis decided to go and watch the play rehearsal, which had been rescheduled for early evening. The improvement was amazing, and when Millie came across and sat beside her on the bank, she told her so.

'You are coming to see the whole thing next week, aren't you?' Millie asked her anxiously.

'Yes, of course — Sally and John and myself will be watching on Sunday afternoon,' she promised. 'Is your mother coming?'

'I'm not sure — I hope so.' Millie frowned. 'She helped me with my costume, anyway.'

'Then I'm sure she'll be there,' Annis told her.

* * *

Yet again, Annis found the following week a trial. She was still covering for the same girl, and although the work was easy enough, she found it frustrating. Part of her wanted to be in Heronsbridge, although she was also very apprehensive about the future.

On Wednesday, her mother rang her.

Her parents had been staying with Annis's aunt in Scotland, so, apart from very brief chats and postcards, she hadn't heard much from them for a while.

'Annis,' her mother said. 'It's been such a long time since we caught up with each other, so your father and I are thinking of coming to London over the bank holiday weekend to see you. We can go to a show — do some shopping . . .'

'But I won't be around!' Annis interrupted her mother and filled her in on what had been happening in her life recently. Her mother sounded so disappointed, to say nothing of incredulous at what Annis was doing, but Annis had a sudden flash of inspiration.

'Look, why don't you come down to Heronsbridge? I'm sure everyone there would be pleased to see you. Besides, there's a play on at the Mill over the weekend — it's 'A Midsummer Night's Dream,' and I've promised to be around to see it.'

And so it was arranged that Mr and Mrs Fuller would drive to Kent on Saturday morning and stay with Sally's parents for the weekend.

When Annis arrived back at the Mill on Friday afternoon it was to find a much happier Sally.

'There's no wedding today, Annis, so how about a spot of retail therapy at the designer outlet at Ashford?'

'Great, but there's something I need to do first — and, Sally, I'm going to need your support.'

* * *

Madame Cecile was putting the finishing touches to Millie's costume for the play and she looked up with a brief smile as Sally and Annis entered the boutique.

'Is that Millie's costume?' Annis asked. 'She's a very talented girl, isn't she? I've watched a couple of the rehearsals and her dance routine is beautiful.'

Madame Cecile frowned. 'I wish not to encourage her in that direction. I agree she's good at dancing — very agile — and as it's Shakespeare, I'm making an exception, but for my daughter to go into the theatre full-time is unthinkable.'

'Why?' Annis asked, at the risk of incurring her wrath.

Madame's petite frame bristled with indignation.

'I'm surprised you ask that question, Miss Fuller. It's so difficult for young people to find jobs these days and it would be better for her to stop filling her head with nonsense and come here, where she would have a worthwhile career.'

'But if her heart isn't in the dressmaking business, then it wouldn't be right to make her do it, would it?' Sally pointed out carefully.

Madame Cecile glared at her.

'We can't all do what we would choose in life, Mrs Barnes. Has Millie been talking to you? Please don't encourage her. She's young and impressionable and rather immature for her age, and her head's been turned by that young man, Dean. I do not approve of their friendship, but I cannot watch over her twenty-four hours a day.'

'She always seems very responsible,' Annis ventured. 'I'm sure you'll be very proud of her when you see her perform.'

'I'm not at all sure that I shall be there,' Madame Cecile said, tight-lipped.

'Well, we're all coming to support her on Sunday. Mr Freeman will be there as well, and no doubt Mr Hadley and Mr Marsden, too. Are you going to be there, Lara?'

Lara gave a sudden unexpected smile.

'Oh, yes, Vicki's taking me. I know she would collect you too if you wanted to go, Madame.'

'You see, everyone thinks so highly of young Millie,' Sally said. 'But the one person she would really want to be there for her is you.'

A slight colour tinged Madame Cecile's cheeks.

'Well — I will see . . . ' she said, still non-committal, and they had to be content with that.

* * *

After two hours of shopping, during which Annis and Sally both bought a number of bargains, Sally drove them home.

'You're good for me, Annis. I haven't done this in a while and it's just what I needed.'

'Then we must see that you do it more often,' Annis told her.

As Sally dropped Annis off at the Mill, she gave her a mischievous grin.

'I've been dying to tell you something, but I'm going to have to wait a bit longer. Uncle Bryn wants to have a word with you.'

Full of curiosity, Annis went to see Bryn Freeman after supper.

'There's something I want to tell you, Annis — come and sit down,' he said. 'The millinery business should be up and running in two or three months' time, so I'm ready now to consider a new proposal from Tristan. Actually, he's had a humdinger of an idea.'

He saw her expression and chuckled.

'Now, don't look like that! I know he's had some harebrained schemes in the past, but this is one that he and Stella have dreamed up between them. You see, Annis, Tristan, Stella and Ross have always had a wider vision for the Mill, but I needed to be very sure before I was prepared to go along with any of their projects. Anyway, I've run this idea past all three of them, and now I want to sound you out.'

He leaned forward, eyes alight with enthusiasm.

'I've always told Tristan that should he have an idea that encompasses the whole business, and isn't just a whim — like a miniature railway or leisure centre — then he should come to me and I would give it serious consideration. Well, I've considered this idea of his and I like it very much. I think I'd like to give him a chance to show what he can do with it.'

'So what is it?' Annis asked, trying to be patient.

'He's suggested that we have an artist in residence who has a studio in the grounds, and puts on exhibitions and so on.'

Annis was pleasantly surprised as she thought about it.

'It's certainly an attractive idea, but how would it relate to the rest of the enterprise?'

'Ah, well, the conference centre could be used for painting classes and the artist would be on hand to do sketches at weddings, or portraits before and after the event. What do you think?'

'I think it's got distinct possibilities,' she said, with a sigh of relief, and she found herself telling him all about her worries concerning the wedding business.

'So you see, I was so convinced that Stella, Tristan and Ross were planning to close down 'Something Borrowed, Something Blue' to make way for some other major project like — oh, I don't know, a casino or a huge sports and leisure complex, or something like that.'

Bryn took her hands.

'Annis, I would never allow anything to interfere with 'Something Borrowed, Something Blue'. Sally has also expressed her concerns, but I had no idea that the pair of you were feeling so insecure about things. Whatever I choose to do in the future must — and will — fit round our present ventures. There — does that reassure you?'

She nodded, her eyes shining as she realised that all her doubts were totally unfounded and that everything was going to be all right from now on.

'We didn't want to bother you with all our problems, Bryn.'

He sighed.

'I've been neglecting my responsibilities, haven't I, young Annis? Since you've been here, you've shown me that. Well, all that's at an end. In future, if ever you, Sally, or any of my other staff have any worries, you're to come to me. After all, that's what I'm here for and I'm definitely not ready to be put out to pasture quite yet!

'Now, while you're here you can help me complete yesterday's crossword puzzle. It was an absolute stinker!'

The Most Important Wedding

Annis's parents arrived late on Saturday morning, just as the first wedding reception of the day was getting underway. Annis took them across to see Bryn, who was expecting them for lunch.

Bryn had Ross with him. It was the first time Annis had seen him in a fortnight and she felt her heartbeat quicken.

He was his usual charming self as she introduced him to her parents

'Ross is staying for lunch — and you, too, Annis,' Bryn told her.

'But I'm helping Sally with the weddings,' she protested.

'There'll be plenty more,' Bryn said firmly. 'Don't argue, lass, it's all arranged. Stella's lending a hand, in any case, so you can spare an hour or so.'

Annis knew when she was beaten.

She glanced at her mother, and saw the expression on her face as she looked at Ross.

'It's uncanny, isn't it, how much Ross resembles Andrew?' Annis remarked.

Her mother looked startled, as if she had read her mind.

'Well, yes, but Ross has broader shoulders and his hair is a darker colour and I think his feet . . . '

Annis looked at Ross and they both dissolved into laughter.

'My mother always notices people's feet,' Annis said.

'Honestly, Annis!' scolded Mollie Fuller, looking embarrassed.

'Well, that's where my brains are,' Ross told her and winked.

Sally's father was soon involved in a conversation with Ross about his travels in America, while Bryn, Annis and her mother chatted about what changes they had noticed in Heronsbridge and at Heathercote Mill itself.

The meal passed all too quickly and the Fullers, anxious not to wear out Bryn, took the hint when Annis and Ross got up to go, and left at the same time, saying that they would sit in the garden for a little while before leaving.

Both of the wedding receptions were finished by early evening and Annis and Sally drove over to Sally's parents' bungalow for supper.

The two girls spent a thoroughly enjoyable time with both sets of parents, watching some old family videos that Sally's father had filmed years before.

As Annis was getting ready to leave, her mother drew her to one side.

'Annis, that nice cousin of Andrew's — I was wondering — is there anything going on between the two of you?'

'No, Mum, we hardly know each other,' Annis told her firmly, but — judging from the quizzical look on her mother's face — she doubted she believed her.

* * *

On Sunday morning, Annis went for a swim and found Ross already in the pool. He waved to her and her heart raced, but then she thought of Stella, who she had seen the previous day, looking more elegant than ever and smiling as if she were the cat that had got the cream.

'We could have our breakfast outside,' Ross told Annis as they climbed out of the pool a half-hour later. 'See you on the terrace in fifteen minutes!'

It was quiet on the terrace for it was still early and there weren't many people about.

'I love this time of day, before all the rush starts,' Annis commented.

'So do I, even though it's a bit of an effort to get up sometimes.' Ross smiled at her. 'Vicki tells me you were quite right about her sister causing problems for the wedding business.'

'Yes. It's just a pity that no-one believed Sally. She's very hurt.'

He had the grace to look chastened. 'Would you believe me if I told you how sorry I am?'

'It's Sally you should be apologising to,' she told him, buttering a croissant.

'And I will, I can assure you. You've made me think seriously about the way things operate here, and from now on I intend to make sure that everyone gets a fair hearing and that we all pull together as a team.'

He paused.

'I'm sorry I wasn't around last weekend,' he added.

'Did you enjoy your time with your family and Stella?' she asked and he shot her a surprised look.

'Yes, I did, thanks. I don't get to see them very often. I thought your parents were delightful, by the way. When are they coming to see the play? This afternoon or tomorrow?'

'This afternoon,' she told him.

They ate in silence for a few moments and then some impulse made her say, 'Stella looks happy.'

Ross's expression didn't change.

'Yes, she is. She's had a lot on her mind, lately — a lot to think about. But she's made a decision and I feel sure it's the right one, although it wasn't easy for her — after Andrew . . . '

He broke off as one of the staff came to look for him with a message about a phone call, and, with a muttered excuse, he drained his coffee cup and went indoors, leaving Annis to stare after him, wondering what else he had been about to say.

* * *

The performance of the play was to be at two o'clock, and all the friends and family of the cast had been invited to Sunday lunch beforehand in the conference centre dining-room.

It was a cheerful throng that made its way down to the lake-side.

To Annis's delight, Madame Cecile was there after all, seated with Vicki, Lara and Tristan. For once the little lady was dressed in a vibrant dark red rather than her usual sombre black. Someone had obviously been taking her in hand.

The play was a triumph. Afterwards, the applause was deafening and Millie was called upon to do an encore of her dance.

Annis shot a glance in Madame's direction and saw that she was beaming and clapping as enthusiastically as everyone else.

Eventually, as the actors and audience departed, Millie ran to her mother and hugged her, and then turned to Dean, who was silently standing at her side, and drew him forward.

'Well done, Annis!' Sally whispered.

'Oh, it wasn't just me,' Annis told her.

Both Sally's and Annis's parents had thoroughly enjoyed the production.

'That young girl, Millie — she's very talented, isn't she?' commented Annis's father.

'We think so,' Annis told him. 'Now,

there are refreshments in the conference centre, or shall we go to a restaurant for a meal and a natter?'

'A restaurant would be nice, darling,' said her mother. 'We're thinking of going into Canterbury with Sally's parents tomorrow. We want to take them out for lunch to repay them for their hospitality. Will you be able to join us?'

'I'd love to, but there's a wedding in the morning, and the last performance of the play after that, and I've promised Millie I'll be there. We'll meet up in the evening, though.'

'You work too hard, darling, and so does Sally. Her mother is quite worried about her. Now tell me, who's that glamorous-looking woman talking to Ross?'

Annis looked across to where Ross was chatting with Stella Freeman. She was wearing a strappy, coral-pink dress and had her hand firmly on his arm. She looked radiant.

Annis swallowed.

'That's Stella Freeman,' she told her mother. 'She and Ross — well, as you can see — they're very good friends. I wouldn't be surprised if — if . . . '

Her mother looked at her sympathetically.

'I see. I suppose I ought to have guessed that's who it is, because she's exactly how I imagined her to be . . . Never mind, darling, your knight in shining armour will come along eventually.'

Annis and her parents spent a relaxing evening, just the three of them, in a pleasant restaurant on the outskirts of Ashford, catching up with each other's news.

But Annis kept thinking of Stella, and seeing again the way she had gazed at Ross with starry eyes. It was obvious that she was in love with him and it was surely only a matter of time before the pair made an announcement.

'You're looking a bit peaky, Annis,' her father said. 'Burning the candle at both ends, I shouldn't wonder. Not much of a holiday you've had, by the sounds of it!'

'It's been great being back in Heronsbridge with Sally and Bryn,' she said, 'and I'm feeling just fine.'

* * *

Tristan came to find her the following morning, his arm around Vicki.

'Annis, I kept missing you yesterday. I want you to be one of the first to know that Vicki and I are engaged.'

Vicki smiled, and held out her hand for Annis to inspect her sparkling diamond engagement ring.

Annis congratulated them and was genuinely pleased, though she hoped Tristan would treat Vicki well and stop acting like a playboy from now on.

Tristan winked at Annis and gave her a roguish smile.

'I was determined to pip my sister to the post, because I guess it's only a matter of time before she makes an announcement herself. You've only got to look at her to see that she's madly in love!'

Annis mumbled a reply and left them to enjoy their walk.

She suddenly acknowledged something that she hadn't been prepared to admit, even to herself, until now: she was in love with Ross.

It was all like a bad dream — one from which she wished she could awaken. Why did it have to be Ross that she had fallen for when it was so apparent that he was involved with Stella? Why was it that every relationship she entered into seemed to end in disaster?

The final performance of 'The Dream' was, if anything, even better than the previous day's, and at the end, bouquets were presented. Millie came to join Annis, clutching hers.

'I've had the most brilliant time, Miss Fuller, and guess what? My mother has actually invited Dean for dinner this evening! He'd better not wear his jeans with the rips in them or she'll be sewing them up!'

Millie giggled and, eyes sparkling, danced away to find him.

Watching her enviously, Annis sighed. It seemed that everyone was finding happiness except for herself.

Presently she went to find her parents, whom she'd arranged to meet in reception after they'd said goodbye to Bryn.

They were chatting to Ross.

'Ah, there you are, Annis. We've had a lovely day,' Mollie Fuller announced. 'We'll tell you all about it over supper. Sally's cooking it for us — I don't know how that girl does it. She works so hard.

'Now, you're not to worry about getting yourself to London tomorrow morning. I feel like doing a bit of shopping and Dad wants to look up one of his old pals, so we've decided to stay in London ourselves for a couple of nights. We'll be able to give you a lift there tomorrow, and we can collect the rest of your things from the flat and drop them off here on the way back.'

Ross raised his eyebrows. 'Goodness, Annis, how much more stuff have you got? You've been lugging cases back here for the past three weeks! Anyway, I've got a much better idea. I'm going to London myself at the end of the week, so why don't I bring you and your possessions back with me? That way your parents won't need to interrupt their journey.'

It was the last thing Annis wanted, but she couldn't very well refuse, so she murmured polite thanks, wishing that things could be different between her and Ross.

* * *

It was drizzling the next morning and Annis and her parents got stuck in traffic, making Annis late for work. Fortunately she was given a much more interesting workload for the remaining few days of her notice period.

It was good to be able to see her parents over the next couple of evenings, and on Wednesday she joined them for the theatre

'You take care of yourself now,' her father said as they parted.

'I hope you'll be down to see us before too long, darling,' her mother added.

Annis's friends at the flat took her out for an Indian meal on Thursday evening and, much to her surprise, on Friday she was showered with gifts by her colleagues, so that when she finally emerged from the office building she was clutching armfuls of flowers, bottles of wine, chocolates, and several good luck cards and gift tokens.

Ross was leaning against the Mercedes.

'Goodness, I can hardly see you under that lot!' He opened the boot to stow her presents away.

Annis was uncomfortably aware that most of the office staff were peering out of the window.

'I hope Stella doesn't mind you giving me a lift.'

'Stella?' He looked puzzled. 'Why on earth should she mind?'

'Well, you're an item now, aren't you?' she pointed out irritably. 'She might not like you running about after me.'

Ross gave an explosion of laughter.

'Annis, you really are priceless! An item indeed! Stella and I are good friends — we have been for many years, but we're nothing more, so you can get that idea right out of your head.'

'But I thought — Tristan said . . . ' Her confusion was plain.

Ross took her hand. 'Stella came with me when I went home the other weekend because she had some serious thinking to do. I've been acting as a kind of mentor to her during these past years,' he explained. 'You see, while she was in Canada she met a man who wanted to marry her, but he told her to take her time and she's been doing just that. Now he's over here, staying in London, and he's proposed again. That's why she went with me to visit my parents, so that she could have peace to think about it and be absolutely certain. And now she's made up her mind! She'll be returning to Canada with him soon — as his wife.'

'But I thought . . . '

'It's obvious what you thought, Annis, but you see, I've never loved Stella — except as a brother loves a sister.' He smiled. 'I've always thought that if I wanted to spend my life with a woman, I would know it immediately I met her. I'd nearly given up — but then you came along and I was right — I did know.' He paused. 'Annis, we only met such a short time ago, but I feel as if I've known you all my life.'

She caught her breath, her heart beating a wild tattoo.

'That's strange — that's how I feel about you, too.'

He took a step closer. 'And you know what, sweet Annis? I've fallen in love with you.'

'That's just as well,' Annis said, her eyes sparkling with joy, 'because I've fallen in love with you, too.'

He caught her in his arms and kissed her — a long, slow kiss — while her ex-colleagues watched transfixed.

'I'm not going to rush you, Annis,' he said. 'You can have all the time in the world, but when you're ready, let me know, and we'll get married.'

Her eyes locked with his and then, to the delight of the audience at the window, they kissed once more.

* * *

Madame Cecile had always thought Easter was one of the nicest times of year to get married. And Annis made such a beautiful bride.

Madame Cecile watched her now as she stepped down from the horse-drawn carriage. Her gown was one of Madame's most exquisite creations — buttermilk satin with a delicate tracery of pink and silver embroidery, dotted with tiny teardrop pearls. Annis's upswept hair was covered by a lace veil belonging to her mother and which had been worn by Mollie Fuller at her own wedding. It was topped by a coronet of silk orange blossom, and Annis carried a dainty bouquet of spring flowers.

Ross looked elegant, and devastatingly handsome, in his dark grey morning suit and gold-brocade waistcoat.

Millie, in her role as bridesmaid, was looking extremely pretty in a turquoise dress, and Sally, for once taking part in a wedding instead of organising it, made a delightful matron of honour.

Bryn Freeman came to stand by Madame Cecile's side as the happy pair posed obligingly for yet more photographs.

'They make a striking couple, don't they?' he said, almost bursting with pride. 'You know, it was my dearest wish that Annis would find happiness for herself again. She gives so much of it to others.'

'Yes, she certainly deserves some for herself.'

'All in all, everything's turned out so much better than I could ever have imagined.' Bryn's eyes glistened with emotion. 'Heathercote Mill is my life-blood, and during the past few years it's been slowly ebbing away from me. But now Annis has brought harmony to the place once again.'

Madame Cecile smiled. 'She's certainly done that — do you know what she said when I asked her what she wanted as a wedding gift?'

Bryn shook his head.

'She said that all she wanted was for me to tell Camille that I approved of her doing a dance and drama course when she left school. Well, what could I say? This morning I gave Millie my blessing.'

Bryn beamed. 'I'm so glad, Cecile . . . I'm sure you won't regret it.'

Madame Cecile's eyes also had a little twinkle in them as she said, 'Of course, I did give Annis something else . . . '

'What was that?' he asked curiously.

'When she came for her final fitting she said that her wedding outfit would be missing something. After all, she would be wearing a new dress, her earrings had been bought for her by Ross from an antiques shop, she would be borrowing her mother's veil, but she hadn't anything blue so . . . ' She lowered her voice. 'I have given her a blue satin garter!'

Bryn Freeman chuckled. 'How apt! Something old, something new — 'Something Borrowed, Something Blue'!'

Then everyone smiled benevolently as the happy groom turned to kiss his new bride.

THE END